Long Way Back

Long Way Back

a novel

Brendan Halpin

Villard

New York

Published in the United States by Villard Books,
an imprint of The Random House Publishing Group,
a division of Random House, Inc., New York.

VILLARD and "V" CIRCLED Design are registered
trademarks of Random House, Inc.

Grateful acknowledgment is made to Incomplete Music, Inc.,
for permission to reprint excerpts from "What Do I Get?" by Pete Shelley.
Reprinted by permission of Incomplete Music, Inc.

1-4000-6278-0

Printed in the United States of America
on acid-free paper

www.villard.com

2   4   6   8   9   7   5   3   1

First Edition

Book design by Jo Anne Metsch

620645

This book is for Kirsten Shanks
1968–2003

Long Way Back

IS LIFE IS IN PIECES.

He is sitting on the couch in the basement, with Motörhead's *No Sleep 'Til Hammersmith* on repeat in the changer. I have just finished washing the last of the dishes and doing the last of the clean-up.

Francis is just staring at nothing when I come into the room.

"Do you want me to stay?" I yell.

"Naaah. Listen to this"—he lifts the remote and pauses the CD at the point where Lemmy, the gravel-voiced lead singer and bass player, introduces the song "Motörhead" to the screaming crowd—"Now what the hell is Lemmy saying here? Is it 'just in case'?"

"Yeah, Francis, that's the way I've always heard it."

"What the hell is he talking about? Just in case you wanted to hear this, here it is? Just in case you were wondering the name of this band, here's our theme song?"

"I dunno, Francis."

"He ought to be more clear, is all I'm saying."

"I'll let Lemmy know the next time I talk to him."

Francis manages a wan smile. "Thanks."

"Are you gonna be okay with just Mom and Dad here?"

"Yeah, I'll be fine."

"Really?"

"I don't know," he says. "I think so. Maybe." He sounds kind of small as he says this, and I feel like he's not my younger brother who's actually six inches taller than me and lives across town, but my little brother who is actually little and lives across the hall from me.

I can see that little kid in his face, and I sit back down on the couch and hug him while Motörhead pummels us. I can't tell if that sick throbbing in my gut is concern for Francis or just Lemmy's light-speed bass playing. I suppose it's actually both.

As I reach the top of the stairs, I stop, heave a deep sigh, and pray. "Holy Mother, please watch over my little brother and comfort him. Dear God, please help him, please reach out to him again." It's not much, but it's all I can do.

*I*T IS 1980. I'm fourteen, and, physically, I'm peaking—thinner and more beautiful than I will ever be again. But this isn't really about me. Spring has sprung in the Greater Cincinnati Area, or as Ira Joe Fisher calls it on *Eyewitness News,* "the Tristate."

So it's a really beautiful spring day in the Tristate. The sun is shining, and we walk into St. Bridget's in Mount Lookout. The church is a squat circle built in the 1960s, and as we walk in, Mom tells us once again how she saved spare change all through her twelve years at St. Bridget's School so they could build a new church, and this piece of crap is what they built.

Sometimes when I stay over at Stacey's house we go to St. Monica's on Sunday morning, which is this beautiful old stone church with a ceiling that seems about a hundred feet tall, with Christ seated at the right hand of the father painted on the ceiling and beautiful stained glass. St. Bridget's, though, has sort of abstract, garish stained glass around the round outer wall and a plain wooden ceiling. I can see why Mom is bitter, but I do wish she'd stop saying it over and over.

There I am, in the pew next to Mom, who looks shockingly like I will look in 2003—brown hair in no discernible style turning mostly to gray; shapeless, comfortable clothes, including jeans that scandalize some of our fellow parishioners. Woe to anyone who mentions this to Mom—they are in for a lecture about the parish she worked in in Guatemala, and how the parishioners there were lucky to have shoes to wear to church, and how God loves what's on the inside, blah blah blah. She embarrasses me—I'm dressed like every other fourteen-year-old girl I know—Izod sweater plastered to my chest (which, I do hate to go on and on, but look at the rack on me! What happened?), matching headband, tartan skirt. Next to Mom is Dad, who also wears jeans and a corduroy shirt. I'm seething. This is Easter, for God's sake! Dress up! I know I'm going to hear about my hippie parents from all my preppy classmates at school tomorrow.

Next to me is my little brother, Francis. Francis is just starting to get that awkward, head-doesn't-quite-fit-his-body look of the early adolescent boy. Because I am a sensitive, kind, protective sister, I call him Pumpkinhead. Francis and I get along okay, I suppose. My friends are always telling me about their pesty little brothers making bra slingshots, or putting a tampon in a glass of tomato juice (I actually saw Stacey's brother, Newt, do that. Unbelievable.), and Francis never does anything like that to me. In fact, he seems to really like and respect me. So I pay him back by teasing him mercilessly until I can get him to hit me. Which always gets me in trouble, because I Don't Care What He Did, You're the Oldest and You Should Set an Example.

So here we have another really boring Easter service. It's nothing special. Later, when Francis is a religious studies major, he'll call this the "capes drapes bells and smells" kind of service. So there's incense, and there's Father Mike's Easter Homily: "Today, as Christ is reborn, may He be reborn in our hearts." Blah blah blah. It's a perfectly okay sentiment, I guess, but I swear, Father Mike says the same thing every year.

We go up to receive the host, and, as I always do, I will try to whisper something in Francis's ear to make him choke when we're walking back to the pew. So we're walking back, heads down, chewing thoughtfully, and I whisper, "Hey, does this taste like feet to you?"

I usually get something out of him with a line like this, but Francis doesn't even acknowledge me. We get back to our pew and kneel down, and I steal a glance at him. His eyes are wide open, he's looking heavenward, and he has this big smile on his face. He's male, he's in color, and there's no spotlight on his face, but otherwise he looks just like the girl in *Song of Bernadette*, which the nuns show the girls every year in an effort to encourage us to be virginal visionaries instead of the decidedly nonvirginal partiers the other schools in town know us as.

"Hey! What's going on?" I ask.

He doesn't answer. He's just staring up, and I watch as tears form in his eyes and begin to spill out, rolling slowly down his cheeks, even though he's still smiling. I stare at him for what seems like hours. The tears continue to trickle out, the smile remains, and I swear he never blinks. I feel like I should say something else to him, but I have no idea what to say.

Everybody else is kneeling, heads bowed, munching the body of Christ. Only Francis and I are not looking down. He's still looking up, and I'm looking at him. He's starting to freak me out.

Some more stuff happens in the mass—more blah blah from Father Mike, and then he tells us it's time for the kiss of peace. I'm starting to get really worried—should I whisper something to Mom? Where has my little brother gone? And, though I don't like this about myself, I am fourteen, so I am wondering if any of my classmates are staring at him, if I'm going to suffer socially because my brother's a freak, or if I'm going to become famous in school as The Girl Whose Brother Went Catatonic at Easter Mass.

I really need him to snap out of it now before anybody else notices. Francis and I haven't hugged at the kiss of peace since I was eight and he was six, so we usually have a quick handshake and a quick, embarrassed "peebwiyou." I'm going to enforce this ritual whether Francis wants to or not, so I reach over kind of roughly and grab his hand, which is still clasping his other hand in prayer. And when my hand touches his hand, I feel a physical jolt.

I don't mean that he jumps, and I don't mean that I get a static shock. I mean that I feel something when I touch him that I have never felt from touching another human being, something I will never feel again. Years later when I live in Boston and see those "Danger Third Rail" signs all over the subway that warn you not to be a moron and touch the rail that supplies the electricity that makes the trains run, I will always remember this day. Francis is plugged into the third rail of the world, he's a conduit for the energy that causes the world to exist, and, for just a second, I can feel it too. It's enough to make me jump back in my seat and bump into Mom, who hisses, "Clare, if you can't behave in Easter mass, you are losing your phone privileges for a month!"

Normally I would respond to this with protestations of how this isn't fair, I didn't do anything, or, if I was feeling especially cranky, with a long retort about how if she was worried about somebody embarrassing this family in church, maybe she should look in the mirror before she leaves the house, but today, I don't even say anything.

I turn back to Francis, and he's finally blinking, and he looks at me like he's confused, like he just woke up from a nap. "Peace be with you?" I say.

He looks at me like I've just spoken Chinese, like he understands that I've made words, but he can't quite wrap his brain around what they are supposed to mean. He cocks his head to one side and looks at me for about five seconds, and then he gets that lightbulb-over-the-head look and says, "Peace be with you."

Finally the mass is ended, and we go in peace. As we leave, Mom and Dad have to stop to talk to Father Mike about social justice, about Christ's call to his people to serve the poor, and about what the parish is doing about it, and I am of course mortified that they still don't get that this isn't that kind of parish, go over to the Newman Center and the Franciscans if you want that kind of thing. Francis still looks kind of blissed out—he's not shambling like he usually does. He's walking, don't get me wrong, it's not like he's floating above it all or anything; except that he kind of is.

Finally Mom and Dad respond to my dirty looks and Father Mike's obvious social cues and give up on their conversation. We all pile into the Rabbit, I slump down in the back seat in an effort not to be seen by anybody who knows me, and we drive home.

By the time we get home, Francis has gotten sullen and sulky, and he becomes this big dark cloud over the house all afternoon, and eventually it just gets on my nerves, because I'm the sulky one, dammit, so I wander into his room while Mom and Dad work on some kind of Latin American Easter dinner downstairs.

"Hey," I say. Francis gives me that dazed, just-woke-up look again.

"Huh?"

"What the hell's wrong with you today? What happened to you?"

He looks at me like he's about to say something, but then he just says, "Nothing. I'm just thinking about stuff."

"Come on. You were crying in church."

"I was?"

"Yeah."

"Really?"

"Yes, okay? So what happened?"

"Promise you won't make fun of me."

"I won't." I am, of course, mentally crossing my fingers at this one.

"And promise you won't tell Mom and Dad."

"I promise." No need to cross my fingers—it's all I can do to ex-change pleasantries with them these days, because I am just way too cool for them.

"I . . . I . . . I don't know what happened. It's just . . . all the sud-den . . . I . . . I don't know, and I think I might be crazy, Clare, I don't understand what happened to me, I think maybe something's wrong with my brain!"

"Something's definitely wrong with your brain." He gives me this look he has—a look that says, instantly, you betrayed me after promising not to mock me, I trusted you and you threw my trust away, you are the worst person on earth—and tears are starting again, and I immediately jump back in with "I'm sorry, I'm sorry, it's just a reflex. I swear to God it won't happen again." I mean it. I can't stand getting that look.

He gives me a long look, testing my sincerity. Apparently I pass the test, because he continues. "I . . . I don't know. It's like I left. Like I wasn't there at all, like I was surrounded by—I don't know, Clare, it wasn't like anything else ever. It's not like I could see any-thing, but it was—promise not to laugh—it was so beautiful. It was like the best, most wonderful thing I could ever imagine, except it was *real.* And you know when you have a really good dream, and then you wake up? That's how I feel. Like I'm already losing that feeling that was so great . . ."

I just look at him. I don't know what to say. We've been faithful mass attendees all our lives, and of course Mom and Dad talk fre-quently about God and how we can serve Him and see His face in the stranger, blah blah, but Francis is twelve—he mostly talks about the Reds and *Star Wars.* What do I say to this?

"Oh," is the best I can come up with.

"And . . . and . . ."—and now he's crying, and I can't stand to see him crying, which he's always been able to use against me, but I don't think he's using it against me now—"the only thing I can imagine is that I saw . . . or touched . . . or anyway . . ."—his voice drops down to a whisper—"I think maybe it was God, Clare, I don't know what else it could have been, and I know that makes me crazy, only crazy people see God, Clare, I don't want to be crazy, and I'm really really scared."

Without thinking about being fourteen, without thinking about him being icky and having a huge head, without thinking at all, I go to him and hug him, which I won't do again until I get weepy and sentimental when I leave for college, and I whisper this to him: "You're not crazy, Francis. I felt it when I grabbed your hand. I didn't see anything, and I don't know what you were looking at or anything, but I *felt* it. It knocked me back into Mom."

Francis breaks the hug, and I awkwardly get to my feet as I remember that I'm a teenager and that hugging your brother is embarrassing and disgusting. "Really?" he asks. He's giving me a look that is the complete opposite of the one he gave me before. It's a look that says I am the most wonderful person ever to grace the earth with my presence.

"Really. It was like you were a live wire." There's a long pause, and I'm starting to get freaked out and embarrassed by this whole thing. "You know? Like the AC/DC song?" Francis looks at me. I rev up my best Bon Scott impersonation, which is not very good, and let loose with "I'm a live wiiiiire . . ."

Francis chimes in with his Angus imitation: "Daaaaa-naaaaa!" and smiles. I feel good about reassuring him, but I'm not sure it completely takes. He mopes around the house for a week or so afterward, and we don't talk about it again for years.

*F*OUR YEARS LATER:

Here we are again on the inside of our house in . . . well, we like to say Hyde Park, but really we exist in a kind of nebulous non-neighborhood. Up the hill from us is Ault Park, which everyone acknowledges is in Hyde Park, which is a rich neighborhood where everybody calls themselves "middle class," but down the hill from us is Eastern Avenue, where the people of limited means of Appalachian descent live, which is what we call them because once after I heard Stacey say "white trash" I used the term at home and got a lecture from Dad that I do actually believe peeled the paint on the banister.

Our house is a hundred-year-old wood-frame house decorated like the inside of somebody's hut in Guatemala. This causes me no end of embarrassment, especially because Mom and Dad will start prattling on at the drop of a hat about the beautiful, moving, and occasionally tragic story behind every artifact, every weaving, every little statue that clutters up our house.

But let's head upstairs to find me sitting in my room. I am eighteen. In an attempt to rebel, I became a punk. This will earn me the "Most Changed" title from my classmates on the Senior Superlatives page of my yearbook. I hadn't realized as a hot, Izod-clad fourteen-year-old that my preppiness was the most effective rebellion against my hippie do-gooder parents, though by now the producers of *Family Ties* have clued into this. So—well, again, this isn't about me, but briefly, I'm wearing my Dead Kennedys T-shirt, which did suitably appall Mom and led to a lecture about JFK and the creation of the Peace Corps and how RFK inspired a generation, blah blah. So far so good. But then they had to go and look at the lyrics and find that they pretty much agreed with Jello Biafra's politics. Dad, being a researcher, did some research and actually came home with Minor Threat's *Out of Step* for me. "It's really all about the problem of being an individual in a conformist society!" he said proudly.

So this is me, attempted nasty punk rock kid, and my dad introduced me to Minor Threat. But I'm sitting in my room—I don't know what I'm listening to, but let's say it's the Ramones, who actually do appall Mom and Dad, simply because they perceive them as dumb. "And it's not dumb in a dumb fun way," Mom says, "it's just dumb! Who writes a song about sniffing glue? That's something that slow normals do!" Apparently one of the perks of being married to Dad instead of being his kid is that you can get away with saying things like "slow normals" without getting a paint-peeling lecture.

So I'm sitting in my room, and just for the sake of symmetry, let's say I'm listening to the Ramones' "Sitting in My Room." Did I mention that I dyed my hair jet-black?

And here comes Francis. He's a full six inches taller than when we saw him last. He's a decent-looking sixteen-year-old kid with freckles and sandy hair. I now feel much kinder and more protective toward him. This has nothing to do with his religious epiphany, which he hasn't mentioned since it happened. Well, except that he then decided to become an altar boy, which really made me fear for him, because all of the worst badasses at St. Bridget's are altar boys. I was afraid that Francis would get eaten alive by these little monsters (who figured, accurately, that they could get away with more if they had the cloak of respectability and piety that being an altar boy lent them), because I think Francis did it because he really wants to serve God.

Well, as it turns out, I needn't have worried, because the little monsters kind of adopt Francis as a mascot, and so he avoids the humiliation and ass-kickings that are the typical lot of the sweet, studious boy. I kind of suspect he may have done this on purpose—Francis understands the social hierarchy of St. Bridget's as well as or better than I do—but I've never asked him.

Francis approaches my door, gives a perfunctory knock as he opens it, and comes in and sits down on my bed.

"What's up?" I ask.

"Well, I think I made a decision."

"About what?"

"About becoming a priest."

"Jesus, you're gonna be a priest? Mom and Dad will—well, they'll either cry because they're distressed or because they're so proud of you. I really can't predict this one. But there will be tears."

"No, no no. I'm not gonna be a priest."

"Oh. That's good, I guess. Why not?"

"Well, I went last week to talk to Father Phil."

"He's really cute. Do you think he's gay?"

"Father Phil? I don't know. Who cares? He took a vow of celibacy. It's not like you could date him."

"Yeah, well, Father Mike took a vow of celibacy too, and why do you think Jeanie Rodgers moved to her grandparents' house in Columbus?"

"I know, I know, because she's having Father Mike's alien love child. You'll believe anything, Clare, I swear. It's actually Jim Michaels's baby."

"Shut up! Jim Beam? I mean Michaels? Shut up!"

"Gospel truth. And Father Mike left because his mom in Florida is dying, not because he knocked up Jeanie Rodgers."

"How do you know all this?"

"Altar boys know all and see all, my sister. Anyway, I don't wanna talk about stupid gossip."

"Okay. Do you have any more?"

"Listen, Clare, really. I don't think I can be a priest."

"Okay, okay. Why not?"

"So I met with Father Phil last week, and I told him I was think-ing about becoming a priest—"

"When were you gonna tell me? Oh, right, I'm only your only sister—"

"—and he said that being a priest wasn't just about mass and the host and everything, that there was a lot more to it, like visiting the sick and fighting with the music director and trying to see people you really didn't like as brothers in Christ, even when they lie about their mothers being sick so they can go to Florida."

"Wait. You just told me that Father Mike—"

"He didn't say anything about Father Mike. He was just giving an example." My brother, by the way, is totally full of shit and grinning ear to ear here. He just loves the fact that he's scooped me twice in five minutes. "Anyway, Father Phil told me I should pray about this for a week and come back to see him. So today I have to go back."

"And, um"—I'm really afraid here that Francis has had yet another vision, that my brother is really some kind of prophet or else lunatic, and that he heard the voice of God telling him not to enter the priesthood. "So, uh, what did your prayer tell you?"

"I don't know, Clare. I mean, I don't know if this has anything to do with God or not." Well, that's hopeful. He seems to have veered away from Joan of Arc territory. "I mean, well, every time I closed my eyes and tried to pray . . ."

"Yeah?"

"I just thought about Meg Sweeney."

"Meg Sweeney? That little tramp? Francis, she's worse than her sister, who I know for a fact is a big tramp, because there was this party at—"

"I know, I know! Meg Sweeney is a little tramp! Why do you think I'm thinking about her all the time?"

This is actually a level of intimacy we've never attained before. Is it made possible by the secret we shared about his Easter vision? Or is it just a natural function of us being together here all the time while Mom and Dad save the world and attend community meetings and parish meetings and won't spring for cable?

I mean, Francis doesn't tell me about the boner he got thinking about Meg Sweeney, or the fact that he is tortured daily by her sexiness (she's like a kid with a new toy—hey! I have breasts!—and by the time she's twenty, she'll be buying new toys for her two kids, which of course I don't know here in 1984 but probably could have predicted). But still, there's an admission here that he is a sexual being.

I am too, of course, but I have done my best to conceal the fact from everyone under this roof, especially after . . . well, anyway, that's not part of this story.

Now, when I was sixteen, I would have teased Francis about masturbating to images of Meg Sweeney, and the thought seriously crosses my mind here, but I am two years older and more mature now, so instead I come back with "Francis, you can do so much better than Meg Sweeney."

He gives me the look again—the "you are the greatest human being alive" look. I've long since decided that it's worth being nice to him just to get these from time to time. He's getting older too, though, and he quickly conceals the look and says, "Jeez, Clare, I'd be happy to even do worse than Meg Sweeney at this point."

NE YEAR LATER:

I am home from college in Boston for Christmas break. I am sitting on my bed again, but the room is much smaller. This is because it is Francis's room. Well, it's my room now, but he took my rightful room when I went to college.

So I am sitting in this glorified walk-in closet that Francis always used to sleep in, and Francis bounds in, not even bothering with the perfunctory knock.

"Hello! Knocking? Ever hear of it?"

"Look! Look!" He's got two orange pieces of paper in his hand.

"What is it?"

"Ramones tickets! I got us Ramones tickets, Clare, we're going to the Ramones!"

This is embarrassing, because I am a legal adult at this point, but I believe I actually squeal. And hug him, and muss his hair. I am psyched to be going to see the Ramones, but I also feel a certain amount of pride at Francis's excitement. I introduced him to the Ramones, and he has come to love them as he loves nothing else except for God.

That's not a joke or some kind of hyperbole or anything. The kid prays all the time, goes to mass every Sunday, still serves as an altar boy, and loves the Ramones. And he's just gotten us tickets.

"Good old Jockey Club," I say as I look at the tickets. I went to many a punk rock show there while I was in high school, always toting a ludicrous forgery of a Missouri driver's license. "You got an ID?"

"The altar boy connection comes through!" he says, and flashes what appears to me to be a perfect facsimile of an Ohio driver's license bearing Francis's picture and the name "Mike Hock." This shows it to be the work of Vincent Travaligni, one of Francis's fellow altar boys.

"Is Vinnie still walking around school going, 'Everybody wants Mike Hock, you can have Mike Hock for twenty-five bucks'?"

"Yeah." For some reason this never gets old to Vinnie, and he's oblivious to the implicit homoeroticism in the fact that he only ever gives "Mike Hock" to boys.

So we lie to our parents and say we're going to the movies. They wouldn't care about me going to a seedy club—indeed, Dad is always encouraging me to "go out and meet all of God's people, even the kind of gross ones"—but Dad would have a fit about Francis breaking the law with this fake ID, and neither one of us wants to hear Mom's opinion of the Ramones again. We drive the Rabbit across the bridge into Newport, Kentucky, which is a depressing, run-down little city full of seedy strip clubs, boarded-up store-fronts, and the only place in Greater Cincinnati where it's possible to see punk rock.

We park, and I say a little prayer: "Dear St. Francis and St. Clare, please protect us, your namesakes, and keep our junky old car from harm so that Mom and Dad don't kill us. Amen."

On the sidewalk outside the club there are sixteen-year-old kids smoking cigarettes—Marlboros for the boys, clove for the girls—and we push past them and head over to the bouncer, a skinny guy who looks about nineteen and spectacularly unqualified to actually bounce anybody should the need arise.

I give him my ticket and show him my actual legal ID, because I am now nineteen, and he says, "Thanks. Enjoy the show. Hey, haven't seen you here in a while . . ."

"I've been away," I say, deciding not to engage in flirtation with an emaciated would-be bouncer, and stand there as Francis, who, though he is seventeen, looks much more like himself at fifteen than Mike Hock at nineteen, shakily hands over his ticket and ID.

The bouncer looks at the ID. "Ah, Mr. Hock!" he says, and I see terror on Francis's face. "Several of your brothers are already inside! Enjoy the show!" And in we go.

The club is a dark, dingy, but fairly large room. The legend goes that there used to be big band dances here, and gambling and liquor during Prohibition, and that the little balcony where the sound guy sits is where they had a guy with a tommy gun to keep all the drunken gangsters in line.

I have no idea if any of that is true, but it certainly looks like the place hasn't been renovated since Prohibition. I look over at Francis, and he is wide-eyed and open-mouthed.

"Close your mouth, Francis. Try to be cool," I stage-whisper at him.

"Hey, I'm cool, Clare, I'm cool. Um . . . can you just go right up to the edge of the stage there?"

"Yeah, if you want, but people are going to be slamming right behind you."

"Slam-dancing? Like on *Quincy*?" I love the kid, but I may have to kill him if he keeps embarrassing me.

"That episode is kind of a sore subject around here"—any random punk will rant at you for ten minutes straight about that stupid *Quincy* show with the stupid Hollywood fake punks, and how slamming isn't about stabbing people, it's about the scene, blah blah blah. I know this by heart because so many of them do it unprovoked— "so please try not to mention it and quit asking me dorky questions."

"Okay, okay. It's just that I'm excited. So that stage, right over there, that I can just go walk right up to, is where the Ramones are going to be?"

"Yes, and that's a dorky question. Go stand over there and save yourself a spot. I'll be back here."

So Francis goes off and plants himself at the front of the stage. I stand in the back and fend off three guys who hit on me and eventually spot Beth, who I used to see here all the time, and we stand in the back chatting and feeling old. Those of us who can legally enter this place are definitely a minority of the audience.

Suicidal Tendencies play, and I watch the back of Francis's head as slammers crash into his back. I can't see his face, but he's still upright, so I guess he must be okay. The snare drum breaks before they can play "Institutionalized," and they skulk off the stage in well-earned shame.

After a few minutes, the lights dim, and the blue and red lights around the stage come on, and dry ice fog starts pouring across the stage. The Ramones come out, and I see Francis right at Dee

Dee's feet. "Jesus, they're fat!" I say to Beth, which is true—
Dee Dee is sporting a noticeable gut, and Johnny's basset-hound
face is jowlier and basset-houndier than ever before. They launch
into "Durango 95," the instrumental from *Too Tough to Die*, which
seems like a funny choice of an opener to me, but I can see Francis's head bobbing right up there next to the stage. More people are
now slamming more violently, so Francis is taking quite a beating
up there, but he is hanging in like a trouper.

And then I see him do something that should embarrass me but
instead really touches me. He reaches up and touches, gently and
sort of reverently, the top of Dee Dee's black Chuck Taylor high-
tops.

The rest of the show is a blur, as all good Ramones shows are, and
afterward we are walking back to the car, and I say, "We are so
busted. We smell like clove cigarettes, beer, and piss. Are we gonna
tell them there was a party at the movies?"

And Francis doesn't even hear me. He is walking along in a
trance. "Hello? Francis? Can you help me with a cover story here?"

"Wow, Clare."

"What?"

"That was just so amazingly cool! It's like I was out of myself. I
mean, I could tell those guys were running into me, and I had a
wheel from the bottom of an amp or something poking me in the
gut, but I was like, part of the music. I wasn't myself—I was just
part of everything."

I stop walking and look at him. I'm a little nervous. All my friends
have given up on going to mass, and I still go and I still believe because my brother touched me while he was part of God, or seeing
God, or whatever the hell happened. It's never been repeated as far
as I know, and I suppose somebody skeptical would say he had
some kind of seizure or something, but that's not what I believe in

my heart. So my faith rests in large part on the fact that I have the memory of the energy flowing through Francis knocking me into Mom. I suppose if my faith depends on physical proof, it's not much faith at all, but it's all I've got. If Francis got the same thing from the Ramones, I'm in for a crisis of faith that will either end with God doesn't exist or Dee Dee Ramone is God, neither one of which is especially attractive to me.

"So . . ." I venture. It's been five years. How do I ask him this? Should I ask him this? "Was it . . . like . . ." This is as far as I can get, and I'm hoping he can fill in the awkward silence

"Was it like what?"

"You know . . ."

"What the hell are you . . . oh! No! Not at all."

"Okay." We walk a few steps in silence. Tomorrow it will seem absurd that I ever panicked about this, but right now I'm relieved that I don't have to contemplate the divinity of Dee Dee.

"And, um, teenage runaway."

"What?"

"We met her in the parking lot of the movies. She asked us for a ride to the Lighthouse runaway shelter, and she smoked the whole time."

"No way. Mom and Dad will want to take her a casserole or something."

"Right. Well, how about we decided to go at the last minute to Rock for Sanctuary, which was a benefit for Salvadoran refugees."

"Like Mom would ever not know about something like that happening."

"Okay . . . so we call and say we're hungry and we're going to the Chili Company for a late-night five-way, and they shouldn't wait up, and then we just pray that they don't."

We get back to the car, which is unscathed, and when we get in,

I say, "Holy St. Francis and St. Clare, thank you for your protection of this vehicle, and if you could make Mom and Dad sleepy, we'd really appreciate it."

"Amen."

*S*EVEN YEARS LATER:

We're in Boston. I came here for college and Francis followed. Mom and Dad went on a church-sponsored mission to Peru to farm guinea pigs, or to Nicaragua with Catholics for Justice to work on a worker-owned coffee plantation, or possibly back to Guatemala with some Dominican friars for that goat-farming thing. They do all of these things, but I don't remember in what order.

I'm working as an ER nurse, which means, yes, I majored in nursing, and yes, I was a complete failure as a young adult rebel. Mom and Dad are both very proud of me, and they tell me in every letter from Central America how much they appreciate the fact that I'm doing God's work in Boston while they try to do His work in Central America. Dad once sends me this: "Christ said we should see him in the stranger, and by helping and comforting people in their times of greatest distress, you are serving Christ every single day. Remember this when you face patients who annoy you, who disrespect you, and who make you want to hurt them—you are doing great work, and I pray every day that God's love illuminates everything you do." I post it on my fridge, and my roommates roll their eyes behind my back, but when I get home from a late shift trying to wipe the memory of something horrible out of my brain, I like to see that message before I reach for the ice cream.

I'm sure you can see that my butt is already much bigger than the last time you saw me, which is at least partially due to all those late night ice cream raids. Tonight I have traded shifts so that I can go see the Ramones with Francis again.

I meet him outside his apartment—he lives with three other guys in a shithole in Allston that I won't even walk into anymore. We can walk to Roadrunner from here. It's a pretty small club, but not even in the same league as the Jockey Club. That is to say, on Thursday nights, they have some sort of disco night for the European club kids here, whereas at the Jockey Club they had a nightly disco for rats and roaches.

We head into the show, showing our actual real IDs this time, and suffer through an awful opening band called King Flux. Then it's the same drill—the dry ice, the lights, "Durango 95"—only something's different. "Hey!" I yell at Francis. "Did Dee Dee lose weight? He looks great!"

"No!" he says. "That's C.J.! Dee Dee's gone!"

"Dee Dee's gone?"

Now Francis is looking at me like I'm the one asking embarrassing questions. I am horrified to realize that he's right. I'm only twenty-six! How did I get uncool already? "Yeah, Clare. They replaced him with this guy."

"Wow!"

The show continues, in a blur, but it's just not the same. Certainly it sounds exactly the same—it's not like Dee Dee's mastery of the bass was such that he's irreplaceable—but it's just not the same.

We leave the show and head over to Mr. Wong's for a late night snack. Working weird shifts in the ER has totally screwed up my eating patterns and driven me into the evil embrace of Ben and Jerry, and I'm ravenous. I'll use these years of working wacky shifts as an excuse for my weight gain long after I stop working in the ER.

Mr. Wong's is a tiny, bright white hole-in-the-wall place where you can get (for example) lo mein on Styrofoam plates for about four bucks.

"So," Francis says as he slurps up some lo mein, "what did you think?"

"I dunno. It made me feel old. And no Dee Dee—I dunno. It felt kinda empty. I'm surprised you wanted to go if you knew Dee Dee wasn't going to be there."

"Yeah, well, I guess it's a kind of a loyalty thing. I mean, I'm loyal to what they meant to me in high school, and I'm going to keep going, even though I don't feel it like that anymore."

"Mmm." I slurp some of my own lo mein.

"Hey, Clare, I guess I should tell you something."

"What's that?"

"I'm leaving school."

"What? You're what?" Francis is in graduate school, going for a doctorate in religious studies. He's told me he wants to focus on ecstatic religious experiences. He's always doing something like this— just like in the middle of a random conversation, he'll bust out with some piece of really important information. It drives me nuts.

"Yeah, well, I just . . . it hasn't even been that long, and I'm already sick of reading about it and talking about it. It's not . . . I guess I thought it would bring me closer to God, but it's not. And it hasn't helped me make sense of . . . well, you know. And Mom, anyway, has been kind of disapproving, like I should be living my faith instead of just studying it. Dad, you know, has been much more supportive, but I think maybe Mom's right. I mean, if . . . I mean . . ." He looks embarrassed, and I guess he is—it's been twelve years, and he's still never told anybody but me about it, and even with me, whenever it comes up, which is rarely, it's almost like it's so private that he can only just barely stand to talk about it. "Whatever that was, and, I mean, I do think it was God, nothing else makes sense, you know I did some research on all the brain stuff . . ."

"Yeah, so did I. You don't have any of the other symptoms."

"You did?"

"Francis, I'm a nurse. I have some contact with medical information. Yeah, I looked all that stuff up."

"Why didn't you ever tell me?"

"It's not like we talk about it all the time. It feels funny bringng it up, like I'm asking you about your masturbation technique or something."

"Well, I find that the water-based lubricants . . ." He's smiling.

"Ick. Ick, ick ick, never ever say the word 'lubricant' to me again. Ack. You are grossing me out. Talk about God again, will you?"

"I've got brand preferences."

"Stop! You were telling me about why you were leaving school, and now you're being gross to try to change the subject."

"Okay. Let's say just for the sake of argument, and also because it's what I happen to believe, that that was God."

"I believe that too."

And again I get the look that reveals me to be a wonderful person, which is something I think only Francis believes. "Why didn't you tell me that?"

"Same reason, and I swear to God if you start talking about masturbation again, you're gonna need a straw to eat the rest of that lo mein."

He laughs. "Okay, okay. So if"—he's whispering now, to shield our conversation from the other, mostly drunk patrons of the restaurant—"God touched me or whatever He did, I don't think the point of that was for me to go off and study the experience for the rest of my life. There has to be a reason behind it. I don't know what it is, but research isn't helping me figure it out. So I'm just gonna take the master's and do something else."

"Whoa. Wow! When did you decide this?"

"A couple of months ago, I guess."

"Months! Months! Jesus, Francis, you never tell me anything! Anything else I should know?"

"I broke up with Nancy."

"What? When?"

"Like three weeks ago."

"I swear to God! I ought to beat you with a lo mein noodle!"

"Well, you've been busy." So I feel a twinge of guilt here—I'm young and single, and I pull a lot of double shifts, and I'm so exhausted that I usually sleep on my off days and don't answer the phone.

"Okay, but you . . . Jesus! You're like changing your whole life, and I'm finding out so late! You're always like this!" He doesn't say anything. He just kind of looks at me. "Well, I hated Nancy anyway."

"I know. You did a terrible job of hiding it." I have to stop and think about this. I was sure I had been perfectly nice and polite to her.

"I did not! I was totally polite to her!"

"Yes you were. And that is how I knew you hated her." Well. There's no winning with this kid.

*T*WO YEARS LATER:

I've given up the ER, and my butt continues its path to world domination. I got sick of the stress, and sick from the stress. Mom and Dad actually kind of made me quit: they came to visit me and I guess I was in kind of shockingly bad shape, and Mom said, "Clare, God needs you too much to let you wreck yourself doing this. Maybe it's not for you." Dad was more direct—he hit the papers and the hospitals and presented me with a list of thirty nursing jobs available in the Boston area.

I interviewed in pediatrics and radiology, but I eventually chose a job with a visiting nurse agency specializing in hospice care. I think this was at least partly out of guilt for giving up the ER—if I couldn't help people not die, the least I could do was help make their dying easier. The pay's not as good, and I have to drive all over the earth visiting dying people, but it's much nicer work. I get to sit and talk to people and comfort them while they're dying instead of fetching things for doctors to ram into them to keep them from dying.

I'm sitting in the basement of St. Teresa's, in the parish hall where they have bingo on Tuesday nights. There's red and black linoleum on the floors, a statue of the Virgin over in the corner, and several inspirational posters with Bible verses and nature photographs hanging on the walls. It's Wednesday night, so it's youth group night. Francis sits in a circle of chairs. He's wearing a Ramones T-shirt, and he's surrounded by about fifteen teenaged boys and girls.

Father Tim told me that the size of the youth group has doubled since Francis took it over. I'm glad, because I kind of forced Francis into this. He was, and is, working as a customer service representative for an exterminator (this apparently being what a master's in religious studies prepares you for), and I just couldn't stand it. He actually seemed fairly contented, though he did stop being able to eat in restaurants. Every time I suggested going out, he'd say, "Oh, Jeez, Clare, not that place. We handle their rat problem, and we're out there every week." He's told Mom and Dad that he just needs time to do some brainless work that isn't taxing him, and they have been very good about accepting that and haven't even mentioned anything to me about being worried about him or anything. But Mom and Dad are thousands of miles away and don't have to have their noses rubbed in Francis wasting everything that makes him wonderful, so I have taken on the role of meddling busybody to try to get Francis to do something a little more valuable than keeping the rats out of Chez Michel. So I talked to Father Tim and got Francis hooked up as the youth group leader.

I'm here to talk about what it's like to work with people who are dying, to see death if not every day, then certainly every week. Francis thinks it's a good thing for the kids to learn about. I watch him do his opening shtick, and I'm just so proud of him. The kids are paying attention to him and not wearing that sullen "My mom made me come here" look that I wore to youth group on those occasions when Mom was able to make me go. Francis also just loves talking about this stuff, and it shows. He's lighting up the room.

"Okay," he says, "so as I promised you, my lovely and talented sister, Clare, is here to talk about her work with the dying." I wave nervously at the group, and one smart-ass boy goes "Hello, Clare! Welcome!" really loud.

"Uh, yes, uh . . . hi," I manage.

"So before we hear from Clare, I wanted to just wrap up our conversation from last week, because we kind of got cut off." He turns to me. "Last week we talked about something that happened during the Rwandan genocide—how gunmen broke into a girls' school and ordered the girls to split up by tribe, and they told them they were sisters in Christ, and they wouldn't divide up."

"Yeah, tell her what happened then," a girl wearing the uniform of the high school misfit—in this case, funky thrift store clothing and too much mascara—says in an annoyed voice.

Francis looks kind of sheepish. "Well, because the girls wouldn't divide up, they, uh, they killed them all." Groans and eye rolls from the group.

"Aagh, Francis, that story totally sucks. I can't believe you're bringing it up *again*," a skinny boy with glasses says.

"Well, you guys got pretty agitated about it last time, and I wanted to give you an opportunity to ask any questions or just sound off about it, because it was right at the end last time when Angie asked what happened to them. So. Anybody have anything to say or ask?"

There is silence, and the teens all gaze downward. Francis lets it drag on and on—it's starting to make me really uncomfortable, but Francis is looking like the picture of serenity. He's obviously prepared to wait them out, to make them break the silence.

Misfit girl raises her hand again. "Okay, since we obviously can't do anything else until we ask a question, why do you think they did the right thing? You went on and on about what a great thing they did, but it was actually pretty stupid, because if they did the supposedly wrong thing and did what the guys with the guns said, at least half of them would still be alive."

"I guess I just think that if they had agreed to divide up, they'd be buying into the rationale for the genocide. By refusing to divide up, they gave this incredibly powerful witness against the evil going on around them."

"And their reward for that is getting shot."

"Well, God doesn't promise us physical safety. He just promises to be with us." This occasions more eye-rolling and grumbling from the teens.

Another boy raises his hand. "Can we *please* talk about something else now?"

"Yeah, okay, okay, fine, I just didn't, you know, I wanted to make sure if anybody had anything lingering from last week, they had a chance to sound off. So, on to cheerier topics. Here's my sister, Clare, to talk to you about dying!"

Now everyone is looking at me, and I'm embarrassed again, not to mention annoyed at the horrible segue.

"Well, now that Francis has everybody in a good mood, let me tell you about what I do." I talk about the care I give to the dying, and I guess I am either boring or making them uncomfortable, because they start to shift in their seats after about five minutes.

Francis comes to my rescue: "Okay, Clare, let's get into some of the juicy stuff. Can you tell when somebody's dead? Like, do you see their soul depart or something?"

"I have to say no. Or, I mean, not usually. Sometimes—I mean, there's the obvious physical stuff, but sometimes you do just get that Elvis has left the building feeling." No reaction from the kids. They've probably never even heard of Elvis Costello, let alone Presley.

"Has your work made you less afraid of dying?"

"Not at all. When I have a patient who is a young woman, I think about all the things I have to live for, all the things I haven't done yet, and I do get scared that I'll be next, sure."

"When you say young, how young are we talking about? How old was your youngest patient so far?"

"Uh, nineteen." This provokes an audible gasp from many of the kids in the group. "He had non-Hodgkin's lymphoma, which is usually pretty curable, but not in this case. I took care of him for about six months." The misfit girl raises her hand. "Yes?"

"How did he take it? Was he like really mad?"

"You know, he was actually much less like that than a lot of people I have worked with. I mean, I have had patients who were fifty years old who were kicking and screaming the whole time. But Elvin wasn't like that. He got into this zone of kind of acceptance that, I have to be honest with you, I don't think I would have had in his position. I mean, I don't think I would have that if I got a terminal diagnosis now, and certainly at nineteen I never would have been able to accept it."

"Why do you think he accepted it?" the kid with the glasses asks.

"I honestly don't know. Some people do and some people don't."

This seems to give the kids something to chew on, and some other kids ask me if I believe in the soul (yes), if I think extreme unction is necessary (I don't think so, but it's brought tremendous comfort to some of my patients), and what I think I've learned from working with the dying (not sure, so I bullshit something on the fly). Finally Francis wraps us up with a prayer, and the teens file out.

"Ugh, I'm sorry, Francis, that sucked. You are so good at this, I have no idea how you do it."

"No, you weren't bad, Clare—it's just that death makes them really uncomfortable. It makes me really uncomfortable. That's why I wanted you to come—I kind of wanted us all to have to rub our noses in it for a while. I guarantee you they're gonna be talking about it next week."

"You are such a liar, but I really appreciate it."

"I'm not lying! I swear! I'll tell you next week, and I swear to St. Francis that I will tell you the truth."

"Okay. Those kids are quite something, huh?"

"Yeah, I really like them. They're always asking the hard questions, and most of them don't seem to mind that I don't really have any answers. I guess my hope is that I can just show them that you can recognize these questions and wrestle with them and still have faith."

TWO YEARS LATER:

I'm in a white dress, and I am looking really good. We're in St. Teresa's, the same church where Francis is the youth group leader and we are both parishioners, and I'm about to get married.

Chris and I met at this church, and I love him, and this should be the happiest day of my life, but right now I am in tears, and Mom and Dad are looking kind of helpless. Even now, as I'm sobbing that my wedding is ruined, ruined, I think I know that I'm just venting some of the stress that comes from planning an event with my mom when she is in another country. We were pretty much on the same page in terms of this being a traditional church wedding, which was a pleasant surprise, since I kind of expected Mom to suggest that we get married in some funky way involving nakedness and acoustic guitars, but we've just been getting on each other's nerves for weeks.

And then there's the business with the bachelor party, which Aunt Mary just had to stop by and report on while I was getting ready. Apparently . . . well, it's probably not as bad as Mary suggested, but let's just say it's incredibly gross and is making me question my judgment in marrying this guy.

Francis, tuxedo-clad, pokes his head in. "Hey, how's it . . . oh."

Even through my tears, I can see Mom and Dad giving Francis these looks like he has to do something. So he comes over to me, puts his arm around my shoulders, and whispers in my ear, "I'm going to say a little prayer here. Okay?"

"Oh . . . okay," I blubber, and close my eyes.

"Okay. Dear God, we thank you for this day, and we thank you for the gift of love. I ask for some comfort for my dear sister so she can enjoy her special day. Amen."

"Amen." And the tears have stopped. His serenity is infectious.

Eventually it's time for us to go, and Mom goes up to be escorted to her seat by one of Chris's acne-faced nephews, and Dad and I are left alone.

And now *he's* crying. "I just want to tell you, before we head up there, how much I love you and how proud of you I am. I just look at you and I can't believe that Mom and I had anything to do with the creation of such a wonderful person. I thank God every day for letting me be your dad."

And now *I'm* crying again, but this time it's much nicer. "Thanks, Dad. Thank you."

"You're welcome. You ready to get married?"

"I guess so."

"Okay. Remember not to lock your knees when you get up there. You could pass out."

"I know, I know."

"Bitter personal experience talking here, sweetheart."

"I know."

We walk up the aisle, and the minute I see Chris standing there, literally shaking and looking at me like I am the only woman on earth, I decide I can probably forgive him his bachelor party indiscretions.

Of course, at the reception, Chris's brother, Allen, gives an incredibly appalling toast that I won't repeat, particularly as it references said bachelor party indiscretions. It's one of those horrible, tone-deaf toasts that has everybody squirming in their seats and threatens to kill the entire party. I paste a smile on my face, but I can't believe I've married into a family that includes this incredible lunkhead with his overlong, unfunny toast, but then again it was my own Aunt Mary who felt the need to come and rat Chris out to me in the first place. And then Francis taps his spoon on a glass, so Chris and I kiss, and he stands up, and he says this: "Well, St. John tells us that Jesus' first miracle was turning water into wine at a wedding feast. And I've been thinking about that a lot today, and so I went and reread the chapter, and it's kind of strange, in that nobody but the servants and the apostles know that a miracle has taken place. But when the wine that Jesus has just miraculously made appears, all the wedding guests start praising the bride's father. They're like, 'Everybody else serves the good wine first and then the rotgut, but here we are, halfway through the feast, and you're bringing out wine that's better than what you started with!' Now, of course, nobody should expect such miracles here"—laughter, and Dad's face turns red—"but I think there are two important messages in here for Clare and Chris. One is that at a wedding you start with something ordinary, and you transform it into something wonderful. Father Tim did that when he made you guys into a family just now. But also, and I think this is just as important, Jesus dispels the fear that marriage is a long slow decline from the passion of your falling in love. This is what people fear, I think, about marriage—that the wine only gets worse as the evening wears on. But here's Jesus showing us, the first wine was good, and what comes after is even better, is not just good wine, it's miraculous wine, it's wine from God's own winery, it's literally priceless. So please raise your glasses and join me in wishing Chris and Clare many many long years together. The best is yet to come."

Everybody raises their glasses, and the evening appears to be saved. And I think for a minute that it's kind of a shame that Francis didn't become a priest.

ONE YEAR LATER:

Please don't even look at my butt. I'm in my house. I've moved with Chris to the suburbs, which turns out to be better for my work anyway, because most of my patients live in the suburbs, so I can avoid trying to drive in and out of the city eight times a day.

This works great, and my house is much nicer than the place I lived in in the city—you know the house, there are thousands of them in every suburb in America—nice, clean, three bedrooms up, kitchen living room dining room strange sitting room nobody ever sits in down, finished basement—it's not where I ever saw myself living, but I'm happy here.

It's Sunday afternoon, and Chris and I are watching football. The phone rings, and I just kind of know it's Francis. Francis is doing well, mostly. After three years of my incessant nagging, he's finally

leaving his customer service job. He's gotten some kind of gig working for the archdiocese as a youth coordinator or something. He's
still going to do his group at St. Teresa's, but now during the day he's
going to be doing—well, I can't really understand it, but I know it
doesn't pay shit and he won't be dealing with angry exterminator
clients.

I pick up the phone, and Francis says, "Oh my God, I just met
the best woman, oh my God, I mean it's not like I doubt the existence of God, but this woman I swear is the proof. Oh boy, I think
I'm in love." Now, this is actually Francis's typical beginning-of-
relationship exuberance, so at this point I'm really barely listening
to him as at least half my attention is still on the football game.

"So tell me the story," I say.

"Okay. So I was hanging around after mass, because I had to
check in with Father Tim about the youth group trip to that World
Food Project farm, and this woman was just there, and, I don't
know, she was also asking Father Tim something, and he introduced us, and then he kind of slinked away. I actually think he was
trying to set us up!" I know for a fact that Father Tim takes this pa-
ternal interest in Francis and is always trying to set him up. I know
this because I am always nagging Father Tim to set him up even
though I don't live in the parish anymore. I'm glad it finally took,
because Francis has been dating these girls he meets at punk rock
shows, and when the whole practicing Catholic, youth group leader
thing comes out, it's usually just about over for that particular relationship, because it's just not very punk rock.

"So what's her name, what's she like, what's she do?"

"Her name is Lourdes, she's an oncology resident at Good Sam,
she's twenty-seven, she is incredibly hot, she's, um, we went for coffee and just started talking for a long time, mostly about like our
families and stuff, I mean I talked about Mom and Dad saving the
entire Spanish-speaking world, and I actually tried to dust off my

Spanish, which I think was pathetic but she found kind of charm-
ing. She's Puerto Rican by way of Hartford, where her dad runs
some kind of insurance company or something. Apparently he does
all the company's commercials. She says she hates going anywhere
with him because I guess if you watch Univision or Telemundo he's
like a big celebrity figure or something. Did I mention that she's
hot?"

"Yeah. You did. Well, it certainly sounds like you hit it off. What
kind of music does she like?"

"Well, I don't know, I mean, she doesn't seem like she's that into
music, and she didn't know who the Ramones were."

"She didn't know who the Ramones were? And you want to date
her?"

"Yeah!"

"Thank God. Because I gotta tell you, those girls who knew who
the Ramones were were just not getting it."

"I know, I know, I know. We had coffee for two hours, did I mention that? She gave me her pager number, and I paged her like five
minutes later and she was like, 'This is Dr. Cordero, I was paged?' "

"Jesus, Francis, don't stalk her."

"I'm not, I'm not. But oh my God that was so adorable. 'This is
Dr. Cordero.' Anyway, she thought it was cute, she wasn't annoyed,
and we're having dinner tomorrow, even though I have to go eat in
the Good Sam cafeteria because she's on call."

"You're eating out?"

"It's not really out, just a cafeteria."

"Yeah, but I mean, was Good Sam an extermination client?"

"Yeah, Ed said they have one of the worst roach problems he's
ever seen. And I don't care, because that is where my beloved
works, so I will eat bad roachy food and then crawl across broken
glass if I have to."

"Yeah, I think they had that moat of broken glass taken out."

"Well, that's good. So it'll just be the roachy food then."

"Yeah. Well, congratulations, Francis. I hope it works out."

"Gah, don't jinx it!"

"Okay, I mean, I'm concerned. It doesn't sound like she's right for you."

"Much better. Thanks. All right, I gotta go shop for an outfit or something, I can't show up for dinner in my Hüsker Dü shirt."

SIX MONTHS LATER:

We're in my house again. Mom and Dad are back from Guatemala or El Salvador or something, and they are staying here. Dad has been great—he reads a lot and occasionally starts an enthusiastic conversation about something he's been reading and seems completely oblivious to his surroundings. Mom, on the other hand, is just exuding disapproval of my bourgeois suburban home and its lack of furnishings handmade by worker-owned cooperatives of indigenous people.

I am also pregnant (so of course my butt is even bigger than before. I'm not ashamed, though: I'm a symbol of beautiful fertility!), and grumpy, and very tired of Mom's stories of the heroic peasants of Central America who pop their babies out, shove them to a full breast, and head out for fourteen hours of work in the coffee plantation.

Francis and Lourdes are coming to dinner. I am looking forward to having someone else here to take Mom's attention for a while, and also to meeting Lourdes, who I only barely believe in.

I've seen Francis fairly regularly in the last six months, and he's been to dinner here twice, both times promising to bring Lourdes and then showing up alone with apologies about how she had to work.

I did receive a very nice card on both occasions asking forgiveness for her rudeness, and I sent cards in return saying, essentially, don't worry about it. This is the only thing that has convinced me that Lourdes actually exists; I know Francis would simply never think of doing something like that.

I am making Chris cook. I am a little nervous about the impression this is going to make. Chris is an enthusiastic but not very skilled cook, but my back is killing me and I don't feel like standing in the kitchen for any length of time. Also, my mother is in there preparing some indigenous specialty.

The bell rings, and I open the door to find Francis and Lourdes standing on my stoop. Francis looks largely the same as ever—gangly, handsome—but is also substantially changed. He is dressed, well, nicely. That is to say, he is pulling off a look that I would probably refer to as "smart casual": a nice collared shirt, pants that are not made of denim, and some very nice black shoes that do not appear to be made of canvas or have a star on the ankle. I stand there slack-jawed. Francis definitely comes from the "God loves what's on the inside" school of fashion pioneered by our parents, and when I have seen him dressed up in the past, that has meant jeans with no holes in them and slightly wrinkled polo shirt.

Lourdes is wearing pants I recall lusting after and dismissing as too expensive in the Ann Taylor at the mall and a top that must have come from the same place. I immediately wonder how this is going to play with our parents: she has the positive factor of being a Spanish speaker, but she dresses like someone who has money. I have to hope that the Spanish cancels out the Ann Taylor, or it's going to be a very long evening.

She's petite—probably a full foot shorter than Francis, and she has long brown hair that she's wearing in an unadorned ponytail. Here is what charms me, though: she's not that beautiful. That is to say, she is perfectly fine, and I would even say cute, but I don't see in her the ravishing goddess that Francis is always talking about. This is just so sweet (and, okay, I'm sure my hormones are kicking in here) that I immediately start to well up.

So I go from stunned silence at Francis's appearance to sentimentality at Lourdes's appearance in about two seconds, and meanwhile they are still standing on my stoop looking at me. Finally Francis pipes up with "Hello? Clare! Humans bearing wine here!"

"Oh my God, I'm so sorry, I . . . um . . ." I turn to Lourdes. "It's really great to meet you, and I don't know what you've done to my brother's wardrobe, but please keep it up."

She smiles. "Thanks. I told him that, you know, when I get to be the head of oncology at Mass General, I can't have him showing up at receptions in some Ramones T-shirt." Okay. There is much to love here: one: she seems to be thinking long-term and not, like Francis's previous girlfriends, to her next paycheck from the used clothing store; two: she is obviously crazy about my brother; three: she's said "Ramones" like it's a Spanish word—"HDDRRamonace."

"She knows it's 'Ramones,' " Francis offers. "It's like a joke we have."

Hee hee! They are so cute!

I take the wine, bring them to the living room, and flee to the bathroom while Francis hugs and introduces her to our parents. When I return, I am relieved to see that the Spanish-speaking seems to have outweighed the Ann Taylor, at least temporarily. Mom is chattering away in Spanish, and Lourdes is either skillfully feigning interest or is actually interested.

Dinner ends up being a very nice, very relaxed time, as everybody chats amicably. Francis tells us he's afraid of pissing off the Cardinal with his new youth program because it's about examining the causes of homelessness, which he thinks might step on the toes of the wealthy businessmen the Cardinal likes to hang out with. I am waiting for Mom to chime in with her favorite line about how they say you're a communist if you ask why the poor have no food, but Lourdes jumps in:

"I can't stand that guy. He hangs out with these guys, goes to BC football games, and I have to step over eight homeless people to get into the hospital, and ten to get into our parish. He has all this power to mobilize the church to be a positive force for social change, and he wastes it hanging around with rich fat guys watching football. He told Francis he'd rather have him work on partnering youth groups with the shelters, which he's already been doing for like three years. Ugggh!"

Well, I am now certain that Lourdes would have to attire herself in solid gold in order to piss off my parents. As for me, I wouldn't mind so much about the solid gold. And just to look at Francis's face, she is shining like the very sun itself, so solid gold would probably be unnecessary.

As luck would have it, Chris's food is actually palatable, and Mom's plantains are delicious. After dinner, I corner Francis in the kitchen, where he's washing dishes.

"Oh my God, Francis, she's fantastic!"

"Yeah. She is. I honestly don't know why she likes me so much, but I'll take it. I even . . ."

"What?"

"You're going to think I'm corny."

"Francis, it's way too late for that, so you might as well tell me."

"I said a special prayer of thanks to St. Bernadette. I mean, she's a big deal to us parish youth types anyway, but I just thought it was appropriate. I thank God every day for her."

I suppose I should explain that Bernadette, virginal visionary of *Song of Bernadette* fame, had her virginal vision in the town that bears the same name as Francis's beloved. I hope I don't need to explain how sweet this is.

ONE YEAR LATER:

We are at Lourdes's house. It's a clean, fully gut-rehabbed brick townhouse in Mission Hill near the hospital district. This is one of these neighborhoods that have a lot of nice houses, and some, like this one, are beginning to gentrify, while others remain in a state of semi-skankiness. This one is nice enough on the outside, and gorgeous on the inside. Everything is clean, the furniture is modern and beautiful, the kitchen has granite counters and gigantic stainless steel appliances that bear brands I have never even heard of.

It has really been Lourdes and Francis's house for at least six months, but Francis is still maintaining the fiction that he lives in his own apartment, apparently because Lourdes's parents, who purchased this house for her when she was in medical school, would not approve of her sharing it with a man other than her husband.

So, appropriately enough, we are here for their engagement party. Well, actually, the party isn't until tomorrow, but Chris and I volunteered to help erase all traces of Francis's presence, which means carting a bunch of clothes and CDs back to the shithole in Brighton that Francis moved into a year ago and never sleeps in.

Of course, I am toting my infant son, Thomas, in a Snugli, and, yes, I am pregnant again, so keep thinking fertility goddess here. (Though Chris and I have agreed that we, like my parents and his, are going to defy the Church and cap our fertility at two offspring.) So, essentially, Chris is going to be the one doing the hauling. He has been a grumpy pain in the ass about this, but he's doing it anyway because he is crazy about me.

Lourdes answers the door wearing sweats, and I hear the Ramones booming from somewhere in the house. "Hey, Clare, Chris, thank you so much for doing this! How's my little nephew?" Tommy greets Lourdes by spitting up on the hand that she's used to chuck his chin.

She laughs and says, "Nice to see you too, buddy!"

"So where's Francis and the offending evidence?" Chris asks.

"Follow the cacophony," Lourdes says, and Chris heads down to the basement. Lourdes and I settle into the living room and Tommy plays on the floor pretty happily. Lourdes takes a call and speaks oncologese into the phone for a minute, which I tune out while I play with Tommy, but then I tune her back in as there's this long pause. "I know. I know. I'm so sorry. I really am. Yes. No. Not necessarily. Okay, I am going to tell you something. That is not true, and the statistics aren't about you. Do you know what I mean? You are not a statistic, and how your body responds to treatment and how tenacious your disease is or is not has nothing to do with some woman from Dubuque ten years ago. I know. I can only imagine. I'm so sorry. I will. Okay." She hangs up the phone and looks at me for a second. I recognize the look she's giving me, because I see it all the time in my work. It's the "I'm really upset right now, but dammit I will compose myself" look.

She takes a deep breath and blows it out very slowly. "I'm sorry, Clare. I have to make a call. I am going to need to swear. Would you like me to go in the other room?"

"I don't think it's going to be any worse than what Tommy hears at home. I figure we can worry about the swearing when he starts repeating it back to us."

"Okay. This will only take a moment."

She punches the buttons on her phone, and the woman who looked like she was about to tear up a minute ago is replaced by this fierce little she-bear, as her soft face hardens up and she growls into the phone. "Dr. Cordero for Dr. Light. When will he be available? Fine, give me his voice mail . . . Dr. Light, this is Dr. Cordero. I just had *another* patient call me in tears after a consult with you. I have no idea what personal issues you have that make you be cruel to women with a serious illness, but we're up to three now, Doctor, and your complete lack of professionalism is impairing my ability to do my job. Talking to you directly hasn't gotten me anywhere, so I'm now officially going through channels."

She punches the phone again and looks at me. "Fucking radiologists. They love their machines, can't talk to people worth a shit." Two more deep breaths, and her face softens again. "Speaking of which, I've been working when I have family over. I'm sorry."

"Don't worry. It sounded important. And all I can talk about right now is poo and puke anyway."

"Well, all I can talk about is ductal carcinoma in situ and Dr. Fucking Light, who is going to have a small but very expensive pump with a rather pointy toe halfway to his small intestine the next time he sees me."

I laugh. I'm glad Lourdes is on our side. "Uh, so let's talk about the party. Is everything ready?"

"Oh my God, I am freaking out. I mean, not about the party, that's all set, but I'm just stressed about my parents coming. I love them, but they kind of drive me crazy. And I think my dad is unhappy that Francis isn't Puerto Rican."

"Did he say that?"

"No, not at all, but you can just tell. It's come out more as stuff about why isn't he a doctor, does he plan to go back to school, wouldn't he like to get an MBA, this kind of thing. But I did tell him that Francis works for the archdiocese and so we might be able to get the Cardinal to officiate, and that seemed to calm him down."

"Jeez, would you want that? Doesn't Francis hate the Cardinal? Don't you hate him?"

"Well, Francis has this strange ability to see his good side, but, yeah, I think he's an incredible asshole. Still, I think it might go a long way toward getting my dad to cut Francis some slack. You know, I mean my dad would certainly prefer the Pope officiating at my wedding, but if he can get the Cardinal, he'll be happy for a while."

At this point, Francis and Chris emerge from the basement laden with garbage bags. "Jesus, Francis, you don't even own that many clothes!"

"Apparently I do now. Well, we're off to my hovel. Love you, honey!" and he smooches Lourdes. I feel a little pang, because Chris and I have been co-workers at the baby-raising factory for the last several months, and this kind of constant lovey-doveyness seems very far away. I miss it. Francis turns to go, and condoms start falling out of a hole in the bottom of one of his garbage bags.

Lourdes and I look at each other and just start laughing.

Francis, at the door, turns back and says, "What?"

"Honey, you're leaving a trail of Trojans."

"Way to hide the evidence, there, Francis," I say. Francis turns purple and picks the condoms up, and he and Chris are on their way.

Eventually they return and we all get pizza and beer (well, those of us who aren't infants or pregnant and lactating get beer, while I have a caffeine-free soda and a Big Gulp of envy). Francis starts going on and on about this bike ride they took the last time they went to the Cape.

He hauls out the pictures, and there they are, all decked out in real biking gear, including the spandex shorts, which is really something I never expected Francis to put on. At least he's got his Motörhead shirt on.

"I swear, it was so beautiful, it was like the sun was just starting to dip at the horizon, and the beach was deserted, and everything was like red and purple and it was just so amazingly beautiful," Francis says.

"Yeah, and the teens having sex were beautiful too," Lourdes adds.

"You don't know that! They were just snuggling under a blanket! It was cute!"

"Nobody looks that guilty when they're caught snuggling, and I really don't think many people snuggle that rhythmically."

"Look, I work with teens all the time—they're just not that bold. They like to keep to back seats and Mom and Dad's bed in the afternoon and stuff."

"Well, I am a medical professional, and I'm telling you that the best face you can put on that is that they were dry-humping."

We are back the next day, and Lourdes looks far too elegant to have ever uttered the phrase "dry-humping." She is decked out in a beautiful dress that I also saw in Ann Taylor, where I know I can never afford to shop with an infant and another on the way, so I now just browse in order to price my soon-to-be sister-in-law's wardrobe.

Francis is actually wearing a suit, and not the ill-fitting, rumpled wedding-and-funeral suit that Dad bought him when he graduated from college, but an actual suit that he looks comfortable in. I know that by now I should stop being amazed, but I can't.

There is some kind of backgroundy jazz music playing, which I know for a fact Francis can't stand, but which definitely suits the occasion more than anything he owns.

Suddenly there is a great commotion outside—a car honking its horn repeatedly, and we hear someone bellow, "HEY! Su familia es nuestra familia!"

I look out the window and see a guy hanging halfway out of the window of a Honda Civic festooned with Dominican flags yelling at a guy in a suit on the sidewalk.

"Well, that will be my parents," Lourdes says. She has told us how every Spanish speaker in America likes to yell out the catchphrase from her dad's commercials when they see him, but I've just seen it for the first time.

Tommy punctuates Lourdes's announcement of her parents' arrival with a rather vigorous and noisy poop, so I take him off to change him. It crosses my mind to hand him off to Chris, but Chris not only helped haul Francis's stuff out of here yesterday, he also had to set foot in Francis's erstwhile apartment in Brighton. When I asked him if it was still a hellhole, he refused to speak of it. "Please don't even make me think about it," he said. "I still have a gut full of pizza, and I don't want to puke all over the car." Tommy never shows any such compunctions, but I guess Chris is just more inhibited. In any case, Chris was my hero yesterday, so I am taking full poop patrol today.

So I'm off changing Tommy, and Mom wanders in, and I am convinced that she's going to offer some sort of changing advice from the foothills of the Andes, or tell me how the noble, guinea-pig-eating peasants she knows never use disposables, but instead she goes, "So how long did it take you to move Francis's stuff out of here?" This is quite eerie given that I've said nothing to her about this.

"Uh, what do you mean?"

"Oh come on, Clare. It's so obvious he lives here. He's just way too comfortable. You can see it the way he moves around the place. Not that I care, mind you. Of course your father and I were having sex for nearly a year before we were married, and—"

"Okay, okay, way way way too much information there. Yes, he's been living here for about six months. Please act like you don't know. I think it's important to Lourdes to maintain the fiction for her parents."

"Oh, I won't say a word. I'm going to be concentrating on trying to get Mr. Cordero to have his company fund the hospital we're working on in El Salvador. I mean, I think a company that does such a huge business with the Salvadorans in this country just has a responsibility to—"

"Mom, keep it light today, please? You'll have the rest of your life to pester him."

"Okay, okay, I'm keeping it light. It's a party!"

"Thank you."

Tommy is clean, and I am able to return to the party for about five minutes and observe Francis and Lourdes holding hands and talking to one of Lourdes's relatives and just looking like they've been together for a million years.

And then Tommy starts to fuss, and about six female relatives from both sides of the family descend on me to give me annoying advice, so I flee to the basement.

I nurse Tommy, and I end up kind of holding court as various people sneak down to see me.

Dad: "She's wonderful, you know. He's a lucky man. Hey, have you ever read Patricia Highsmith? Horrible misanthrope, but there's a lot to chew on in terms of morality and . . ."

Mrs. Cordero: "Your brother is just the kindest man. My husband always wanted her to marry the president or something—although with this president, maybe that wouldn't be so good—can you imagine your shame all over the news every night? But I really think she's lucky to have such a good, kind man who adores her. He told me about his work with the archdiocese. I don't think he knows how important it is."

Francis: "So now I have to go to Hartford next weekend to play golf, apparently."

Lourdes: "Clare, I love your mom, but she needs to stop talking to me about Guatemala. She sends me all her Guatemala e-mail updates, she is up there talking to my mom about Guatemala, and I feel like telling her I don't give a shit about Guatemala! Puerto Rico is not even in Central America, and anyway I grew up in Hartford!"

Eventually I reemerge and give Chris the imperceptible-tooutsiders "let's leave" look, so we go and exchange hugs with Francis and Lourdes, and I look back at them as I am walking out, talking to some cousin or other with their arms around each other's waist, and I'm just so happy for them.

ONE YEAR LATER:

We are in the back of the cathedral. I am technically the matron of honor (matron! Me! Even given how fat I look in this dress, and my baby Dorothy squalling next to toddler Tommy in the front pew, it irks me to think of myself as a matron), because the word came from the archdiocese that the Cardinal would not really dig officiating a wedding at which the best man was female, which only confirmed for me Lourdes's diagnosis that he's an asshole. So I am Lourdes's matron of honor, and Lourdes's brother, Carlos, is the best man.

But here I am backstage with Francis, who is sweating bullets in a tux. He's pacing, drumming with his fingers on every surface, and, when he stops pacing, bouncing up and down on the balls of his feet. "Ugh," he says. "I mean, I just want to run away and be married and not have to do this part."

"It'll be fine, Francis. Here." I pull the CD player out of my bag. "It's *Road to Ruin*."

"Thanks, Clare. Um, do you think? . . . I mean . . . would you pray with me?"

"Of course, goofy!" So we close our eyes, and I guess it's up to me like it was back at the Jockey Club. "Dear God, Holy Mother, Saints Francis, Clare, and Bernadette, we thank you for this day and for the gift of love in our lives. We thank you for Chris, Tommy, Dorothy, and Lourdes, and for all our blessings. We pray that everything goes smoothly today and thank you for the opportunity to celebrate this love together. We ask for good wine at the beginning of the feast, and better wine later on. We ask this in Jesus' name, amen."

"Amen." He gives me that look again, and I feel like they ought to make my fat ass Cardinal.

We sit in silence for a minute, and then I say, "Well, I should get back to Lourdes. She looks gorgeous, by the way."

"Of course she does! That's my bride!" He hugs me, puts on the earphones, and starts listening to "Bad Brain."

The mass itself is wonderful. The Cardinal is, as Lourdes is always telling us, an asshole (Francis, of course, is much kinder: "He has a lot of competing interests to balance, and though I don't always agree with him, I do think he wants what he thinks is best for the Church"): his homily was about their duty to God to populate the earth. He doesn't specifically mention birth control, but his message is clear, and all I can think about is Francis leaking condoms from a garbage bag.

But, as always, the beauty of the mass overcomes the lameness of whoever is officiating it. This is especially true here, where the mass is extra-high because of the Cardinal's presence (talk about your capes drapes bells and smells!).

There is just this moment in every mass—well, it's just . . . there's something about this ritual that really helps me feel close to God and my fellow parishioners, and it's something I have a really really hard time achieving in any other setting. The mass is said in both English and Spanish, which makes me cry, and best of all, my little brother is marrying somebody wonderful, somebody who deserves him and somebody he deserves.

The reception is a blur to me, because of course I still have matronly duties to my own children. (Chris was a superstar during the whole ceremony, but he doesn't have the equipment to nurse Dorothy, so I have to sneak off and be a beautiful symbol of fertility away from the head table.) Toasts are given in English and Spanish, and I really regret the fact that taking French was my big rebellion against Mom and Dad, because I now have a family I can't fully talk to.

Still, I gamely give my toast, though I am haunted by Francis's fantastic toast at my wedding and the knowledge that whatever I say is going to fall short of that. I also just have to hope somebody translates it effectively. It's short and sweet: I say that while I was growing up, I wanted two things: a sister, and Francis to be happy. And now I have both, and even though this isn't my day, I feel very blessed.

TWO YEARS PASS. For me, they are all about diapers, binkies, and horrible anxiety-producing preschool visits. For Francis and Lourdes, they are all about wedded bliss, biking trips both local and international, and increasingly desperate pleas for grandchildren from both her parents and ours.

I appreciate the irony here, because Mom and Dad are especially keen critics of the Church's anti-birth-control policy because of what they've seen in Central and South America. Here in North America, though, their own children apparently have a duty to be fruitful and multiply. Chris and I probably haven't made things any easier for Francis and Lourdes, since we've set a very fruitful example.

I have a patient in Brighton, where the archdiocese offices are and where Francis no longer pretends to live, and so I will be able to meet him for lunch twice a week for as long as Mr. Mok hangs on.

We meet at this nice little pizza place. You know the place—they have real plates and cloth napkins and the booths are not made of Formica, but it's still a pizza place. I obviously should be dining on salad—okay, I'm not as big as when I was pregnant, but that pert fourteen-year-old body I used to have is buried under more layers than I'd like. But I'm still having pizza.

Francis is also having pizza, but he can obviously afford to. He apparently still has his awesome metabolism, and now he is this big bike-riding guy who commutes to work on his bike even when it's snowing, so he is basically a lean machine. I really can't understand how I could come up such a loser in the genetic lottery when we came from the same parents.

"So," I say between bites of pizza laden with olives (yes, I know, more fat grams), "any more pressure to reproduce from Mom and Dad?"

"Well, I wouldn't call it pressure, I think it's just interest. I mean, you know, they're seriously considering relocating here, and I guess they are kind of feeling like they'd like to give up serving God by serving the people of Central America, but somehow they need to have three grandchildren here in order to be able to face their consciences. I mean, I get where they're coming from, so it doesn't really bug me."

This response is both predictable and annoying, which leaves open the question of why I steered the conversation down the "boy, Mom and Dad sure are annoying" road; this only ever succeeds in making me feel petty and small. Before I can backpedal and try to put out a remark that shows that I too am full of love and forgiveness for Mom and Dad, Francis comes back with "Anyway . . . I think I'm ready."

"What do you mean?"

"Well, we've talked about it, and obviously I'm going to be the one who stays home, I mean she makes four times my salary, and I just feel like I've done pretty much all I can do at the archdiocese, and I'm ready to do something else, and I think this is it."

I picture Francis as a stay-at-home dad. It's a good picture. "Well, so you're ready, but how's Lourdes feel?"

"Aw, you know, her career is just heating up, we're still young, she doesn't want to take the time right now, that kind of stuff."

"So . . . I mean . . . is this like a source of tension?"

"Not really. I mean, I knew who she was when I married her, I knew she was ambitious and everything, so it's not like I can complain when I suddenly find out she's ambitious. Whatever. We're on somewhat different schedules about this, but it'll be okay."

Lunch continues, but only for a few minutes, because my pager goes off and I have to get out to Framingham to see Mrs. Carolini.

Mr. Mok ends up being some kind of superhero and living for nearly a year. This is great because it does give his brother time to get the money together to get himself here from Guangzhou, and because it allows me to have lunch with Francis twice a week for a year. This ends up being the most time I've spent with Francis since I got married, and it's a great year in that respect. He hasn't mentioned anything about wanting to have kids or anything since then, and has, in fact, started a new youth group initiative where youth groups from urban and suburban parishes partner up to do community service in each community. There was a little piece about him in the *Boston Globe*. I got it framed. So much for him having nothing more to do in the archdiocese.

It's now Columbus Day weekend. For some reason I can't quite fathom, Francis and Lourdes are not biking the length of the Appalachian Trail this weekend or anything, so they come and spend the day with us. We drive around, pick apples, leaf peep, and come back for dinner.

So here we are in my house. It looks much the same as before, except now the floor in every single room is littered with toys. And we have those plastic safety latches on every cabinet door. And our couch has an array of toddler-induced stains on it. And . . . well, the transformation from nice suburban yuppie house to lame suburban parent house is pretty well complete. Anyway, I'm in the kitchen and I've just put dinner into the oven while Francis and Chris are in the yard playing some kind of game with the kids that appears to involve Francis as a very unconvincing scary monster. This, of course, is just an excuse for the kids to tackle and abuse Francis, which he seems to love for some reason.

Lourdes comes into the kitchen and looks out at the game and says, "Anything I can help you with?"

"Sure—I don't think I'll be able to drink that wine you brought all by myself."

"Perfect. Something I'm good at." She opens the bottle and pours us rather robust glasses. She takes a sip, relaxes, and says, "Not one word of this to your parents or mine, but we're finally trying."

"Trying, um . . . oh! *Trying!*" And here, though I have long since become a real adult with children, a job, and a mortgage, I squeal and give Lourdes a big hug. "That is so great! I mean, that's really great! How's it, um . . . I mean, how long, uh, I mean . . ."

"It's going great. I mean, wonderfully. It's been about two months and no luck yet, but, you know, it's pretty fun making the attempt. Or, I should say, Francis is happier and more attentive than he's ever been, which is saying something. I'm kind of exhausted, though— you know, I've got the charts and the thermometers, and sometimes it's just one more goddamn thing I have to do after I've worked a long day. And it's only been two months, but of course I'm starting to panic about my fertility, you know, I waited too long, I'll never conceive, this is what I get for putting my career first—I actually hear that last one in my mother's voice, because I am so sure that is what she's going to say if she ever learns that I didn't conceive just by thinking about it."

"Ugh. I can imagine. Well, don't worry—I'm sure she'll find ways to drive you insane no matter what happens."

Lourdes laughs. "Yeah, I keep encouraging them to retire to Puerto Rico."

"Well, anyway, this is great news! I mean, you know, it will be great. I mean, I think you guys are going to be great parents."

The kids bellow outside as they bring Francis to the ground. "Well, I know he will be anyway," Lourdes says. "He's always been so great with kids, he's just going to be a fantastic father."

"You'll be great too. You won't believe you could ever love anyone so much."

"I hope you're right. Well, anyway, I have to conceive first." We sit for a minute, and then she asks after Mrs. Murdoch, who was one of her patients and is now one of mine.

We eat dinner, and we talk about their vacation, and Chris and I talk about our work, and I tell the horror story of the preschool from hell that I visited, and after dinner Chris puts the kids to bed and Francis helps me wash dishes while Lourdes answers a page.

"So," I say.

"Yeah?"

"Were you gonna tell me?"

"Tell you what?"

"That you're trying."

"What do you . . . oh." He's blushing. "No, I wasn't going to tell you! I don't wanna jinx it!"

"You're not gonna jinx it!"

"Well, anyway, I don't really want to talk about it, but I will just say that it is very exciting and it's going to be a big change and I'm really excited about starting this new phase of my life."

"Did you finally wear her down? I mean, did you do that sulky thing like you used to do with Mom and Dad?"

"I did not ever do any sulky thing, Clare, that was you who did the sulky thing from age fourteen to eighteen I think, but anyway, no, we don't have that kind of relationship. She told me she'd tell me when she was ready, and then one day she told me she was ready!"

"Just like that?"

"Just like that! 'Hey, let's make a baby,' or something like that."

"Well, I think it's fantastic. This kid is going to be so lucky to have the two of you as parents."

"Well, lucky to have her anyway. I mean, I wanted this and I still want it, but I am terrified I'm going to be a disaster. I mean, I work with these teenagers, and I just hear all these horror stories, and you always read these cranky guys talking about how today's parents are too chummy with their kids, and that is totally going to be me, I am going to be a complete failure and I'll be publicly mocked as the worst parent ever."

"Actually, I think I have that title sewn up, so you'll have to get in line. Anyway, you'll do fine. This is going to be the best thing that ever happened to you."

I PRAY FOR FRANCIS and Lourdes to successfully conceive every day for the next two weeks. During these weeks, Mr. Mok goes into a quick decline, and it gets harder and harder for me to go see him. It's been a year now, and he and I have built a relationship, and I always enjoyed the way he rolled his eyes at his wife's bustling around the apartment, and the cheerful way he took my advice and his medicine.

Once his brother arrived, there was always a festive feel at the Moks' house, as though this were just a family reunion, but now the mood has turned somber. Mrs. Mok is still bustling, and there are always at least four or five children, nephews, nieces, or cousins sitting around looking anxious. Mr. Mok is barely conscious, so I talk only to his wife, who tells me that he mostly sleeps, who worries about the sounds he makes—is he in pain and can't tell them? I tell her probably not, but I don't really know. We give him morphine in an eyedropper under his tongue and hope for the best.

I used to just sit and visit with the Mok family, but now there are diapers to be changed, and always the anxious questions that boil down to this: You're the expert here. How long? How long?

I wish I had something concrete to tell them. I try to duck the questions, because I really don't know, but eventually I come back with "I'd be surprised if he lives out the week." So, of course, he lives out the week, and then another week after that. I am present at the moment of his death, and it is about as nice as a death can be: I am packing my stethoscope and blood pressure cuff into my bag, and Mrs. Mok is wiping his face with a washcloth, and suddenly there's something missing, and I realize it's the sound of Mr. Mok's raspy breathing. Mrs. Mok begins to wail immediately, and the younger relatives all seem to relax at once. I go without thinking to hug Mrs. Mok, and she throws her arms around me sobbing something in Cantonese that I don't understand, but that of course I understand completely.

"I'm so sorry," I tell her. "I'm so sorry."

I make all the phone calls for them, and then, for me, it's off to another dying person. I sit in the car briefly and ask God to take care of Mr. Mok, to comfort his family, but especially his wife, and to give me strength to go help another person who's dying. I sit for ten minutes, and then I do feel like I have the strength.

After this, I am no longer regularly in Brighton, so I stop having lunch with Francis, and we trade phone messages for a few weeks but never manage to connect.

And then, one day, the phone rings.

"Hello?"

"Um . . . Clare?" The voice sounds small and kind of strangled.

"Francis?" Silence, and my panic reaction is setting in. Tommy is standing two feet away from me going, "Mommy! Mommy! Mommy!" and I'm not hearing him, because my heart is pounding and my muscles are twitching. "Francis? Is that you?"

"Yeah," he says and starts to sob.

"Francis, what's wrong? Tell me what's wrong!"

"I . . . she's . . . we're in the hospital and something's really wrong, she collapsed and I thought she was . . . Oh God, Clare, I'm so scared!"

"Okay, what hospital are you in?"

"Good Sam."

"Where are you?"

"Intensive Care."

"I'll be there in half an hour."

"Okay," he says.

"Don't worry, Francis, it's going to be okay."

"I . . ."

"Listen to me, Francis, are you listening?"

"Yeah."

"Holy Mother, we ask for protection and healing for our beloved Lourdes. We ask this in Jesus' name, amen."

"Amen."

"Okay, sweetie, I'm coming."

"Okay."

I hang up the phone and yell at Tommy that he knows not to interrupt me when I'm on the phone and Auntie Lourdes is very sick, and so could he possibly wait with his problem or go ask Daddy?

He goes crying to Daddy instead, and I feel horrible. I go and apologize to him and tell him I'm just very worried about Auntie Lourdes, and Chris wants to come to the hospital too, but I tell him to stay here and put the kids to bed instead.

So I am driving into the city with my heart racing, and I am praying more or less constantly, things like, "St. Bernadette, please watch over Lourdes, Heavenly Father, please save her life, Holy Mother, protect her, Jesus, you fucking moron you cut me off! Fucking asshole!" This last, obviously, is not a prayer, but I find I have no patience for the idiosyncrasies, or possibly just idiocies, of my fellow drivers tonight.

There's no place to park at the hospital, so I have to keep going down down down these concrete ramps forever until after ten minutes I finally find a spot on level five, all the time ranting: "Fucking go home, it's seven o'clock on a Tuesday night, what are you people all doing here, Jesus, you'd think there would be a place to park here, it's a pretty big hospital and everything."

I get out of my car and run to the garage elevators, which take forever to come. And then I have to get out of the garage elevators and walk to the regular hospital elevators to find Intensive Care on the third floor.

The waiting room features a nice little solarium window that now just opens onto darkness, some blond wood couches and chairs with ratty red upholstery, a television carrying a very static-y image of *Wheel of Fortune* with the sound off, and, of course, a feeling of loneliness and desperation. Wherever all of the people parked in the garage are, they certainly aren't here. (Later I will figure out that they are illicitly parking for the Red Sox game, because even the hospital scalps you less for parking than the lots around Fenway.)

Francis is sitting alone on a red couch with his head in his hands. I go over and sit next to him and rub his back. He doesn't look up.

"I'm here, Francis. What's going on?"

"I don't know. She fell over, I mean she collapsed, and she wouldn't wake up, and here we are. I guess they're working on her or something—they told me I couldn't go in."

"Okay, first of all, that's bullshit unless she is actually in surgery right now. Do you want me to raise some hell here? Because I'm happy to do it."

"Yeah, I guess. I mean, I'd like to see her."

I am all prepared to go ballistic on whoever presents themselves, and I'm preparing a speech about how Dr. Lourdes Kelly's husband is out here cooling his heels, and perhaps Dr. Kelly could have the rules bent, and things like that, trying to work "Dr. Kelly" in at least five times. Unfortunately, I don't get the chance, because a doctor emerges, heads straight for Francis, and says, "Mr. Kelly, you can see her now."

Francis all but runs through the swinging double doors to her bedside, and I corner Dr. Rudd, as his nametag with blurred digital photo that could be anyone informs me he is. "So what happened?"

"I'm sorry, are you a relative?"

"My name is Clare Hayes, and I am a registered nurse and Dr. Kelly's sister-in-law."

"Well, okay, it's just the new confidentiality rules—"

"So what happened?"

"Well, I'm afraid the news is not good. It's actually very bad. Mrs. Kelly—"

"Dr. Kelly."

"Right. Dr. Kelly has had a subarachnoid hemorrhage of the brain. The CT scan showed a ruptured aneurysm in her frontal lobe. She actually presented multiple aneurysms, as about fifty percent of patients do, but the rest of them do not appear to have ruptured at this point."

"So?"

"So . . ." And there's a pause here you could drive a truck, or, more accurately, a hearse through. "I'm sorry. That is to say, it is extraordinarily unlikely that Mrs. Kelly—"

"Look, Mr. Rudd, she is a doctor in this hospital, so can you just call her Dr. Kelly?" Somewhere deep in my brain I know that it makes no difference at all what this asshole calls her, but I feel like I may have to kill him if he doesn't acknowledge that Lourdes is a doctor.

"It's unlikely Dr. Kelly will live out the month. The CT scan shows significant damage to her brain. In the unlikely event that she emerges from coma, she will likely have serious disabilities for the rest of her life." Okay, he called her a doctor, and I want to kill him anyway. He is so cold—this is the biggest thing happening in my life and certainly in Francis's life right now, and this guy is just so cold about it. Many of my patients actually complain about the same thing—that doctors get annoyed with you when they don't believe they can help you. It's like you're messing up their stats or something.

The further complication is that I cannot let this man repeat what he's just said to Francis, because I just won't have my brother exposed to this guy anymore. Bad enough he has to live through this. But, of course, this means that the responsibility for telling him is going to fall to me.

I walk through the double doors, and the metal that coats them feels very cold on my hand. I walk into the room where they have Lourdes in bed. It's a normal hospital room: she's lying in bed with an IV in her arm and various wires that feed into the machines at her bedside attached to her head, her chest, and her arms. The floor is speckled linoleum tiles, there is a television hanging kind of precariously from the wall opposite the bed, and there is a large window that offers a spectacular view of the east wing of the hospital and part of a parking garage.

Lourdes looks like Lourdes. She does not have the wasted, skeletal look that so many of my patients have. She looks like maybe she was pulling an extra-long shift and decided to take a nap and got hooked up to all these machines by mistake. I think Dr. Rudd must be insane, he must have made some sort of incredible mistake. All you have to do is look at her to see that she's not sick at all.

Francis is sitting in a chair that is the reclining cousin of the chairs in the waiting room. He's holding her hand, and his head is down. I lean down to catch what he's saying, and he's finishing up a Hail Mary. I wait till he's finished and just bust out with it.

"Um, Francis?"

"Yeah?"

"I talked to the doctor."

"What did he say?"

"Well, she's had a brain hemorrhage . . ." and Francis starts to cry. He's already seen the rest on my face.

"No, Clare, no!" he's yelling as the tears stream down his cheeks. "No, she is not dying, no she is not going to die. I know that's what he said, you've got your bad news face on, but he's wrong, Clare, he is not correct, because my baby is not dying! She's going to walk out of this bed and cure cancer! She is walking out of here and coming home with me! She is not going to die in this bed!"

I don't know what to say. I hope to God he's right, and I can't bring myself to argue the rational point here. Certainly I've seen doctors be wrong before: they gave Mr. Mok six weeks, and he hung around for a year. Dr. Rudd was certain that Lourdes is done, I am sure he is joking with his buddies about sticking a fork in her somewhere even now. But Francis is equally sure. And, at least once, Francis touched, or was touched by, God. So maybe I should give him the benefit of the doubt here.

"I'm sorry, sweetie," I manage, and I hate the way it sounds as soon as it's out of my mouth.

"Don't be sorry, Clare. This is a bump in the road. We're gonna laugh about this with our kids." He is, no pun intended, dead certain and dead serious. He's talking as though he had to explain to somebody that the earth is a sphere.

"Um, okay, Francis. What can I do for you?"

"I'm just going to stay here. Maybe tomorrow you can bring me some clothes or something. And bring her some clothes too. I hate seeing her in this thing—" He tugs at the white johnny with the blue and red squares on it. "Also, if you wouldn't mind calling Father Tim tomorrow—ask him about the guy, I think it's Father

Pete, over at Sacred Heart who does that healing mass thing. We'll probably need him. And, um, can you get me a rosary?"

"Um. Okay . . ." Francis is the only person under seventy I know, or even know of, who ever prays the Rosary. But whatever helps. It occurs to me that I should bring him food too. "Is it okay if I stay here for a little while?"

"Of course. Grab a chair and pray with me." I end up dragging an ugly red chair in from the waiting room, and I come back in the room and find Francis holding Lourdes's hand and bowing his head. I sit and quietly ask God to heal Lourdes, I ask Him for strength for Francis (though he clearly doesn't need it right now, he may run low later on), and I ask Him to take away my fear and my doubt and bless me with some of Francis's faith.

I leave an hour later, and Francis is still bent in prayer holding Lourdes's hand. I stroke her hair and his, and I silently thank God for bringing them together, and I try to ignore the fact that, despite my prayers, I am still terrified.

I GO HOME AND want only to sleep, but first I have a horrible conversation with Mrs. Cordero. As soon as I tell her what's happened, she loses her mind and starts wailing. I feel guilty for having to tell her. I wonder if she'll always hate me because I am the one who told her. Mr. Cordero gets on the phone, and he is all business. He wants to know exactly what the doctor said and what her odds of survival are. He is calling up Web sites on brain aneurysms while he's on the phone with me. He thanks me quietly and tells me they will be in Boston in two hours. I go to sleep, and the next morning, I call in sick from work, take the kids to day care, and get busy. I call Father Tim and ask him about the healing mass. He calls me back in twenty minutes with a promise to have Father Pete in Lourdes's room tomorrow afternoon. I e-mail Mom and Dad in Nicaragua, and I get a speedy reply—they expect to be here within four days.

I head over to Francis and Lourdes's house. It feels very strange to be here. It seems like the house should look different in some way, but it just looks normal—there are dirty clothes on Francis's side of the bed, there is a paperback book lying facedown and open on the night table on Lourdes's side. I grab clothes for both of them, and I find Francis's rosary on top of his dresser. There is still coffee in the coffeepot in the kitchen, so I dump it out. It's nice to have things to do: it helps me to think less.

I find a parking place (level four this time—I'm moving up) and go up to the Wraptacular! restaurant in the lobby and grab us a couple of chicken Caesar wraps and some smoothies. I'm sure Francis hasn't eaten. When I get to Lourdes's room, it appears that Francis has not even moved since I left last night. Neither, unfortunately, has Lourdes. The only difference is that the Corderos are in the room now, with Mrs. Cordero sitting with Francis and praying, and Mr. Cordero pacing. I stand in the doorway for a minute just looking at them. I exchange awkward hugs with both Corderos and head over to my brother.

"Hey, Francis, I brought some food."

He looks up, dazed, as though I've just woken him up, even though his eyes were open. "Oh, thanks, Clare. Did you bring my rosary?"

"Yeah. Here it is." He grabs it and starts praying immediately. I stand there for a minute feeling foolish, but then finally have to interrupt him. "Um . . . Francis?"

He looks up, annoyed, his lips still mouthing Hail Marys.

"Why don't you take a break? Take a walk or something, have some of this sandwich."

"Thanks, Clare, but I really don't want to. I want to be here when she wakes up."

"Okay. Will you at least have the sandwich?"

"Maybe later."

"Okay, listen. I need you to drink this smoothie. You can take a sip between beads or whatever, but you must get some kind of food into you. You don't know when" (of course I'm thinking "if") "she's going to wake up, and you need to be able to stand up and walk out of here when it happens" (it's never going to happen) "which you won't be able to do if you do not put some kind of food into your body. So do it."

I hold out the smoothie, and he takes it and absentmindedly sips before beginning his next Our Father.

"Um . . . Father Tim said the guy from Sacred Heart will be here tomorrow to do some kind of healing service."

"Great. Thanks. Probably we'll be home by then, but it's nice of him to come."

"And Mom and Dad are coming."

"Great."

"Um, is there anything I can do?"

"Yeah, you can just sit here with us for a while. Maybe talk to her. Try to keep the docs at bay. The nurses are okay, but I had to shoo out a bunch of guys on rounds at like six this morning. They were talking about her prognosis . . . they were just talking like she's not even here, like she's just a number instead of my sweet baby."

(But she's not here, Francis, I'm thinking. She's gone already. But he believes, so I will keep trying to do the same. But it's so hard.)

So I sit with them. I try to pray, but my heart's not in it. I just can't find a peaceful place to talk to God. So I decide to talk to Lourdes instead. "Hey, so did I ever tell you the story about Francis and the orange peel? How about you just wake up and I'll tell it to you. Okay, well, I'll tell you anyway. So I'm in the fourth grade, Francis is in the second grade. You know that picture with the cowboy outfit? That's from that same year, right, so picture him looking like that. Mom packs our lunches and mentions to us in passing as she cuts oranges in half that she and her sisters used to eat the orange and then turn the half peel inside-out to make a little doll hat. So we're all at lunch, all the kindergarten through fifth graders at St. Bridget's, and I look up from my Fritos and see Francis walking to the trash with an inside-out half of an orange peel on his head.

"Now, I think I'm going to die of embarrassment, but then I see Sister Anne, who's huge and terrifying, charging toward him. She starts bellowing: 'Do you think that's funny, young man? Do you think that is funny?' Francis starts to cry immediately, and she just stands him there in the middle of the lunchroom and bellows at everyone, 'Attention! This young man apparently thinks it is funny to put an orange peel on his head!' and of course half the place is giggling. 'If you agree with this young man that this is funny, raise your hand! Well? I heard laughter, surely some of you think this is funny!' and of course nobody raises their hands. Well, eventually she lets him go and tells him he has to wear the orange peel on his head the whole day.

"And at the end of the day, I'm waiting for him to come out of class, and five of his buddies have inside-out orange peels on their heads too! He started this mini-revolution! And every day thereafter, somebody would distract Sister Anne while somebody else walked to the trash with an orange peel on their head! It became this total thing everybody did to get over on Sister Anne!"

Well. Lourdes doesn't laugh, and the Corderos don't appear to have heard at all. Francis, though, looks up and smiles. And then goes back to praying. I sit there in silence for a while and then go home and hold Chris and cry and thank him for being alive.

I BARELY SLEEP THE entire night. I toss and turn worrying about Francis and Lourdes and about the fragility of my own family. I hug the kids very tightly as I send them off to day care and start to cry, and Chris explains that Mom is very worried about Auntie Lourdes. He asks me if I need him to stay home.

"No, I don't think so. I'm just going to go hang out at the hospital for a few hours, so maybe I'll catch a nap in one of those incredibly comfortable chairs."

"Okay. I'll bring the kids over at the end of the day, and I'll bring some dinner for you and Francis."

"Thank you, honey. Oh, you'd better bring something for the Corderos too—I'm sure they'll still be there."

"Okay. I'll aim for something a little more upscale than pizza then."

"Great. Thanks, honey."

"You bet. Take care of yourself too, honey."

"I will."

"Okay." He leaves, and I think that was a nice thing to say, but I have to take care of him, the kids, Francis, Mom, Dad, and even the Corderos.

And, as it turns out, Father Peter from Sacred Heart. Father Tim calls me and tells me that Father Peter needs a ride to the hospital, and he's ninety years old, so could I go pick him up at Sacred Heart and take him over there?

Sacred Heart is an old, somewhat decrepit church in Dorchester. It is made of tan stone, and the stained glass windows are covered in rusty wire mesh. The inside is even worse—paint is peeling from the ceiling in large flakes, all of the lights in the foyer are covered in the same rusty wire mesh that covers the stained glass, and the pews have long since lost their finish and look like they might give you a splinter if you looked at them funny.

And then there are the crutches. There are two pillars next to an altar on the side, and they are lined with crutches, canes, and walkers. The crutches on the bottom look like the Tiny Tim model, while the top sports stainless steel walkers and canes and a few crutches that look like they are made from the same stuff as fancy tennis rackets and golf clubs.

As I approach the pillars, I can see that there are many pairs of eyeglasses sprinkled in. Again, these range from the Ben Franklin model on the bottom to some barely visible ones with a big Chanel C next to the lenses at the top.

I am half expecting Father Peter to pop out from behind a pillar and prophesize at me, but, instead, I stand there alone until I find a door to the rectory and walk around going, "Hello? Father Peter?"

"Yes! Come on back!" he says in a deep, hearty voice that doesn't at all fit my preconceptions of how a priest too old to get himself across town should sound. I follow the sound of his voice to a small office. The walls are white and bare with the exception of a large crucifix. He's a tall man with a full head of white hair and a set of stylish glasses. He sits at a small oak desk and types on a computer.

I introduce myself and he grabs a bag next to his desk and a cane, and we walk with agonizing slowness to the car. As we pass the pillars full of crutches and eyeglasses, I can't help but glance at Father Peter's cane and glasses. Unfortunately, he catches me at it.

"I know, I know," he says. " 'Physician, heal thyself,' right?"

"Uh, I uh . . ."

"Oh, everybody thinks it. Let me tell you a story that reveals a great theological truth." I brace myself here for a tedious lecture straight out of my tenth grade religion class. "Once, not too long ago, I was in the convenience store across the street," he intones. "I was making macaroni and cheese in the rectory, and I remembered how a long time ago, I used to cut a tin of Spam into cubes and add that to macaroni and cheese, so I went to the convenience store in search of Spam. They had no Spam, but that isn't the point of my story. The point of my story is this: inside the convenience store, they have an automatic teller machine, and on the day I was there on my doomed Spam mission, someone cursed at the machine and turned to the clerk and complained that the machine had taken his card. The clerk looked over and said, calmly and in a tone that I think bespoke resignation, 'Sometime it work . . . sometime it don't.'"

I laugh in spite of myself (because it has to work, you asshole), and he laughs, and all I can think is that he'd better not tell Francis this story, because Francis needs so badly for it to work.

*W*E ARRIVE AT the hospital and score a spot on level two of the garage. I make Father Peter stop at Wraptacular!, which makes me feel slightly guilty, but I just know Francis won't have eaten, and I feel confident that I can at least get a smoothie into him. I do worry about how long he will survive on the one-smoothie-a-day diet if Lourdes stays in this coma for a while. I also worry about how long Lourdes can survive with no food at all. She's getting IV fluids, but soon she's going to need a feeding tube. I know Francis will insist on them putting it in if there is any hope at all that Lourdes will wake up (or even if there isn't—Francis's hope is clearly much stronger and deeper than anyone else's). I've assisted in this procedure before—it's violent, and there is gagging involved. I don't want Francis to see this done to her. I suppose this is a worry for another day, but I seem to have a hard time breaking my worries up right now.

The curtains in Lourdes's room are wide open, and the gloomy overcast light is seeping in the window. The fluorescent light at the head of Lourdes's bed is the only thing breaking up the gloom, and it gives her a yellowish appearance. There are introductions all around, though Francis can barely be bothered to be polite to Father Peter. I am worried about him. He is pale, stubbly, and smelly. In fact, it is going to get difficult to stay in this room for any length of time if he doesn't shower or at least change his clothes sometime soon.

"Francis," I say. "You need to drink this." He takes the smoothie and begins slurping obediently.

"And you are going home, taking a nap, and showering after the service."

He looks at me like I have just said the stupidest thing he's ever heard. "Of course I'm going home, Clare! We're both going home! She's going to walk out of here with me."

"Well, right, but, um, she'll be pretty weak in any case, and she probably won't be able to leave right away even if"—he gives me the "you are the worst person alive" look at my use of this word, but I soldier on—"she wakes up right away. So do her and all of us a favor and go take a shower. You smell."

For a second here, I feel like I see my brother, my regular brother, not the insane prayer maniac who's been hovering by this bed, come out. He looks at me. "Really? Do I really . . ." He sniffs his pits. "Wow! Okay, I guess I do stink. But maybe I can just wash up here in the—"

"No, Francis. You need to go home. You can take my cell phone, and I will sit right there in your smelly chair and not move until you get back, and I will call you if anything changes."

And my brother sinks down below the surface again, with the worry monster taking his place. "Okay."

Father Peter has taken a little gold container full of the host, a vial of holy water, and a flask of oil out of his bag, and he is kissing a crucifix, and we are ready to begin.

Father Peter prays and sings, and then we all pray and sing, and we pray some more, and then there is more praying, and we are all sprinkled with holy water and anointed with oil, and Father Peter lays his hands on Lourdes and implores the Lord to send His healing power into her, and we sing again, and pray again, and we take Communion. I have to confess that I am initially just going through the motions. I close my eyes to pray and all I can think about is the horror that's coming—the funeral planning, the tears, the burial, and the destruction of Francis's soul. But as the service goes on (and on, and on, and on—it clocks in at two and a half hours), I feel my worry draining away, and I am filled with a feeling that is completely foreign to me—I can call it a blissful calm, but that doesn't even begin to describe it.

I can feel the energy in the room in a physical way. It feels warm and slightly electric. Now, perhaps this state is accessible to anyone who has the discipline to pray for two and a half hours (or, in this case, an hour and a half by the time I'm really doing it sincerely), but it is novel to me. I feel, for the first time in a long time, the presence of the Holy Spirit.

When the service ends, I sit quietly, just breathing. I look over at Lourdes, and I fully expect her to hop out of bed. How could she not? I just feel like if I can calm my brain and reach this kind of benevolent trance state, then surely anything at all is possible, then surely the loving God whose presence I sense in this room is going to grant this woman we all love a second chance at life and she is going to rise and walk.

After ten minutes, I begin to come down, or up, or something— in any case, I regain my worried, petty self, and it is a pretty serious bummer. Even more serious is the fact that it's clear that Lourdes is not rising or walking. She continues to breathe shallowly, oblivious to us all.

Francis sits and stares, and then he begins to cry. He's vocalizing in a way that kind of freaks me out—moaning in a kind of high-pitched way, and going "waaaaaaaaaaa-ha-ha-haaaaaaaaaaaaaaaaaa," over and over again. I go over to his side of the bed and hold him, and of course I start to cry too. After ten minutes, he's able to speak, and he says, "Come back, honey, please come back, please come back, please please please come back," and I am able to walk him into the hall.

Mr. Cordero follows, and I am eventually able to press my cell phone into Francis's hand and get Mr. Cordero to take him home. I sit on the ugly red couch preparing myself to go back into the room with Lourdes and Father Peter and Mrs. Cordero, and Dorothy wakes me up two hours later going, "Mama? Wake up, Mama, wake up."

DOROTHY GETS AN ear infection and wails for most of the night on Sunday night. I am in Lourdes's room a great deal, usually when Francis is being escorted home for his mandatory shower. I buy a large number of smoothies. The elderly Russian woman who works the register at Wraptacular! punches my order in before I can speak and greets me with "How your sister-in-law? I pray for her very much." I appreciate it, but after a couple of days, I just feel like telling her that I'll tell her if anything changes, but right now I just want my smoothie and my salad without the conversation.

Of course, I'm really worried about Francis. At home, in bed, I pray for some sort of reconciliation to the idea that Lourdes is going to die. Some nights I can just about get there—that is to say, I can just about accept the fact that Lourdes is not going to be here anymore, even though it feels like an incredibly cruel loss to the world. What I can't quite get to, though, is peace with the destruction of my little brother. Right now he is surviving only with serious assistance from me and Mr. Cordero, and Lourdes is still alive. What is he going to do to fill up his days if he can't pray by her bedside? Am I going to have to make sure he's eating and showering every day? This feels incredibly heavy on top of my responsibilities to my own children. I owe Tommy and Dorothy and Chris more attention than I've been giving them. Chris is saying all the right things, but I think he's started saying them less enthusiastically. I've told myself it's a short-lived crisis, but what if it's a lifelong crisis? How will I take care of everyone? So I don't know how I'm going to be able to take care of Francis when Lourdes dies, and I don't know what's going to happen to him.

Two days after the healing service, Mom and Dad arrive, and they are so good with Francis and with me that I feel guilty about the fact that I was dreading their arrival. Mom swoops in and takes charge of my kitchen and cooks us food that is delicious, healthy, takes more than ten minutes to prepare, and doesn't come in a box or bag. Dad loves the kids and is perfectly happy to get on the floor and play with them, change diapers, and even watch *Teletubbies*. ("It's a fascinating cross of the futuristic utopia and a rural idyll!" he offers.) Somehow they also manage to take shifts with Francis too, and take some of the "making him eat and shower" burden off of me.

When I first take them to the hospital, the Society of St. Jude is in Lourdes's room. St. Jude is the patron saint of lost causes, the one you pray to for hope in a hopeless situation, and apparently the one who attracts rosary-toting seventy-year-old women in his devotional cult. Their perfume overpowers even the smell of the dozens of floral arrangements that occupy every horizontal surface in the room except for Lourdes's bed.

The old ladies come for an hour every afternoon and pray with Francis that Lourdes may be healed and walk out of her hospital bed. I join in twice. It feels good, though not as good as the healing service. But at the end of the hour, I feel more serene than when I started.

And every day at the end of the hour, Lourdes breathes shallowly and does not notice us.

Sometime during this sleep-deprived week, Francis of course signs off on a feeding tube, and I make him leave while they put it in. I close my eyes, hold Lourdes's hand, and listen as her gag reflex kicks in. It's a horrible sound, but it does allow her to stay alive for a few more days.

I get home late that night, and Dad is sitting up reading in the living room. He's got a glass of scotch next to him, as he does every evening. He's never been much of a drinker, but, he says, "I just can't get this kind of thing in Central America, so I'm going to enjoy it while I'm here."

"What's the word?" he asks me.

"Well, they put the feeding tube in," I say, and I find myself crying before I even know what's happening. Dad gets up from his chair and wraps his arms around me. "How . . . Jesus, Dad, I think, I mean, I just want her to die at this point. Is that wrong? How can this be happening?"

"I don't know, sweetie," he says. "I don't think it's wrong. It doesn't really seem like there's much of her there anymore."

"I know, but Francis . . . he's going to . . ."

"Francis is going to be okay. He's made of stronger stuff than you think. Admittedly, not as strong as you, but he's got an inner strength second only to yours. You won't have to talk him off the ledge or anything."

"I hope you're right. And that was a nice thing to say. I don't feel so strong today."

"Well, you are. Chip off the old block," he says with a laugh.

Finally it's Thursday—it's been ten days since Lourdes collapsed.

I get to the hospital at four and send Francis home for his shower. He leaves, and I begin my daily conversation with Lourdes. "Well, hello there, it's Clare, Francis is gone for a few minutes, but he'll be back soon. So how's your day? Well, Dorothy's been sick with some kind of ear infection, the third one this year, so naturally her pediatrician wants us to put the tubes in her ears, which I suppose is a good idea. I don't know—what do you think, Dr. Kelly? Not telling, huh? Well, I know pediatrics is not your field. I love you anyway. And so does Francis, but you probably know that already. I have seen a lot of very sick people, you know, and I can count on one finger the number of spouses who've shown this kind of devotion. I hope that some part of you knows this. I'm sure you do. So would you like me to talk about Dorothy's poop? We've had a marked change in color and consistency these days . . ." Before I can begin to describe Dorothy's Dijon-mustard-colored, viscous poop of the last two days, Lourdes begins to convulse. Her arms and legs twitch, and her mouth twists into a sideways O. She groans and gurgles. I know that her neurons are just firing, that she's not really here, but this noise is the first vocalization to come out of her since her collapse, and she sounds for all the world like she's being tortured. It's a horrible, violent convulsion, and Lourdes is gurgling and moaning. I'm pressing the nurse's call button and trying to hold Lourdes's hand, but it's jerking all over the place, and I want to call Francis, but he's probably still in the elevator, and if I try to work the phone I can't continue to pound the call button with one hand and grab for Lourdes's twitching hand with the other, and before I can work out how to do this, the nurse comes running in, and Lourdes's twisted, pained face suddenly relaxes, she stops twitching, and she stops breathing. She's gone.

Unfortunately, Francis hasn't signed a Do Not Resuscitate order, so the doctors come in with the crash cart and stick needles into her arms and convulse her body again, this time with electric shock.

They ask me to leave, and I do, but I can tell by their halfhearted looks that this is a perfunctory attempt. They have to be able to say they tried, but there is clearly no hope on anyone's part that this is going to work, and, indeed, I am hoping pretty strongly that it won't. I go out to the waiting room and call my cell phone on the pay phone. I'm trying to work up something to say, but before I can do it, Francis answers, "Hello?" and when I hear the terror in his voice, I choke up, and all I can get out is, "You need to come back."

He hangs up without answering, and five minutes later he is at Lourdes's bedside. I say a silent prayer of thanks to God and to Lourdes herself that Francis didn't see either the convulsions or the attempted resuscitation. All he sees is his sweet wife at rest. I don't know how much of her was here at the end, but I will always believe that she waited until Francis was gone to spare him from seeing what I've just seen.

Of course, since Francis doesn't know what he's missed, all he can do is wail. "Ohhhhhhhhh, my baby my sweet baby, no no no no no NO! No! No! Where is she, Clare, where is she, why did she go? Why did she go when I wasn't here? Why did she go, whyyyyyyy," and he trails off into sobs.

I rub his back and he cries for an hour until the orderlies come to wheel his wife's body away.

SOMEHOW WE GET Francis back to his house. It's not his and Lourdes's house anymore. Francis heads for the couch and curls up in a ball. He's asleep within about five minutes. Mr. Cordero takes Mrs. Cordero, who has been giving Francis a run for his money in the loudest, most sustained howl of grief-stricken agony competition, upstairs. As soon as Francis and Maria are asleep, our parents and Mr. Cordero start planning the details—calling funeral homes, calling the archdiocese to see if the Cardinal is available to officiate at Lourdes's funeral, calling florists.

I make a pot of coffee and clear a space at the kitchen table to drink it. I have to move away ten days of mail addressed to Lourdes, as well as her Good Sam photo ID and her pager in order to find a place to set my mug down. It's funny—I deal with the dying for a living, but once they go, my work is done and I'm out of the house. I never have to go into the house and see all this weird evidence of their existence everywhere. It just seems bizarre: Lourdes's pager is here, and the little red light is blinking—she has seven pages. How can she be dead if she has seven pages?

I sip my coffee and start to fume as I listen to the parents bustle. Mr. Cordero paces through the first floor with the cordless phone, and I hear him saying, "No, I don't need to see it. Your description is adequate, and the price is acceptable to me. Now given what I'm spending on this, I'm going to expect a level of personal service that exceeds what you normally offer. Are you prepared to guarantee me this? Wonderful. And your name is? Thank you, Stephen. Now, Stephen, will you be the person in charge of all the arrangements? Wonderful. And your cell phone number? Wonderful. You can reach me here, and I'm sure my wife will have some questions and instructions. No, she has a preferred florist in Boston. Thank you.

"All right, that's taken care of." He turns to me. "Does Francis have the Cardinal's number here somewhere?"

"I really don't know. Do you think . . . I mean, don't you think you should run some of this by Francis? I mean, I know for a fact that Lourdes hates . . . hated the Cardinal, and I think—"

Mom has wandered into the room and jumps in with "Clare, Francis is a wreck. You said yourself he hasn't slept in ten days. He's not in any kind of position to make decisions right now."

"I know, Mom, but he's going to be . . . he needs to be consulted. His wife is dead. We need to defer to what he wants."

"Well," Mr. Cordero says, "I think your mother is right. I know that Lourdes loved Francis dearly, and I'm trying to do what she would have wanted by protecting him from these people. You must see how funeral directors work, Clare. Do you want to throw Francis to the sharks in the condition he's in?"

"Well, I guess not." I wonder about the condition Mr. Cordero is in, but I guess busting the asses of funeral directors is his way of grieving right now.

"Honey," Mom offers, "forgive me, but you're not in the greatest shape yourself. Why don't you just go home and get some rest?"

"I can't go home, Mom. Francis needs me here." I think but don't say that as much as I think Mr. Cordero may be right that Francis needs to be protected from the funeral directors, I think he also needs to be protected from all these parents. "I'll just head down to the basement and catch a nap on the couch there."

I hear Mr. Cordero talking to the assistant to the Cardinal's secretary as I walk down the spiral staircase to the basement.

Eventually, of course, I do return to my own home. I'm happy that I have Tommy, and Dorothy, and that Chris is not dead. I feel so lucky it's embarrassing. I have everything, and Francis has nothing, and a small part of me is glad, relieved it wasn't me this happened to.

Three days later, we are in the parlor of the Madden Brothers Funeral Home. Stephen Madden, who appears to be about twenty-five, stands at the door in a gray suit looking official and vaguely terrified. Mom tells me that the Corderos have really been making him work for his money, calling him six or eight times a day and two or three times a night. The funeral home is like every funeral home—it's decorated in furniture that is both cheap and excessively ornate. It's got pictures of the Virgin Mary and the Sacred Heart of Jesus on the walls. It's clean, but it feels dusty. At one end of the large room, Lourdes lies in her top-of-the-line casket, done in a tasteful gunmetal gray.

Well, I am taking it on faith that what looks like an emaciated dead whore was in fact Lourdes once. She's wearing one of her best dresses, which is typically simple and elegant, but she is made up like she's going to rise up and head down to the Combat Zone looking for business. It makes me angry, and I hate for Tommy and Dorothy to see her this way. I hate that they are going to remember her this way, instead of as the vigorous, athletic genius she really was.

There is a kneeler in front of the casket as there always is at Catholic visitations, and Francis kneels in front of the coffin sobbing. I did manage to get him into a suit today, and Mom assures me that she's been making him eat, but he looks like hell even for a guy who's sobbing uncontrollably.

The visitors drift in and offer their condolences to the Corderos, to Carlos, to Mom and Dad, to me. Francis continues to cry in front of the casket. It's beginning to get kind of unseemly. I hate that I'm even aware of social pressure in this situation, and I hate even more that I'm planning to act on it even before Mom starts giving me that "do something about your brother" look.

I head over to the kneeler, cross myself, and say a brief silent prayer. I thank God for Lourdes's life, and I ask Him to help my little brother. And, yes, to help me to help him.

"Francis," I whisper.

"Yeah?" he looks at me with dazed, red-rimmed eyes.

"You're totally hogging the kneeler. You need to move it so that people can pray and get out of here. Uncle Ted in particular looks like he might have some serious problems if he doesn't get to happy hour. You don't want a Christmas of '88 scenario here, do you?"

He manages a little smile. "I don't know. It might be a decent distraction. But I just can't talk to people, Clare, I can't do it. I can't talk to every oncologist in Boston, I can't talk to Cousin Trish, I can't do it . . ."

"Oh my God, Francis, Ted has a flask in his pocket. Let's go see if he'll share."

"He does not."

"He does, Francis. Look at the bulge in his pocket! He hasn't been that glad to see Aunt Liz in forty years. Come on. If we're lucky, he's back on Bushmills."

"Clare, I hate whiskey," he says, but he's standing up, and I can almost feel the breeze from the collective exhale of everybody else in the room. I give him my arm, and we begin to walk toward the door as I try to fend off potential comforters with a babbling monologue of, "I'm sorry, he just needs some fresh air, yeah, needs some air, yeah, we're taking him outside, sorry, yes, thanks for coming, Francis just needs a little air, you know how it is, Uncle Ted, could you help me here?" Of course many relatives and co-workers don't get the hint and try to descend on him, but I manage to get him to the door having only endured two smothering hugs.

Uncle Ted pisses me off by denying the flask's existence, but eventually he gives it up, and Francis and I both take long pulls. Francis of course coughs and sputters, but he does seem to be a little closer to a normal state. I make a mental note to find out who the patron saint of alcoholics is and say a little prayer of thanks for Uncle Ted's addiction.

The funeral mass is at the cathedral the next day, and Chris and the kids and I sit with Francis. It's a capes drapes bells and smells affair, and the Cardinal is officiating. I would be angrier about this if it appeared that Francis cared, but, as much as it pains me to admit this, both sets of parents were right—Francis is beyond caring, and it's just as well that they took care of all this stuff for him, even if they made some horrible decisions. The Cardinal gives the eulogy, and it's very nice—he talks about her dedication to serving others, he praises her work (though he hardly needs to—there's a battalion of bald women in head scarves here to attest to the importance of her work), and he touches briefly on the impossibility of understanding God's decisions. I can't really fault any of it, but it just falls so far short of explaining this wickedly funny, strong, driven woman who loved my brother, and it fails completely to comfort anyone wondering why this happened.

We take the host, and, walking back to our pew, I ask Francis if it tastes like feet to him. He turns and gives me a faint smile, which reassures me. He's still in there somewhere. The congregation defers to us, and we walk out and into the waiting limos. Tommy is very excited by the limo, and we let him watch TV. It's a long ride to the cemetery, and I wonder how Francis is doing in the limo with our parents. I wish he was in here so I could comfort him and protect him.

We arrive at the cemetery. It's about forty degrees and drizzling. There's a little white party tent set up right over the hole where they're going to plant her, and the hole is tastefully draped in Astro-Turf. The Cardinal apparently doesn't make trips to cemeteries in the freezing drizzle, so Father Tim is here to say a few words. He says that he did not know Lourdes well, but what he knew of her was that she lived passionately—that she was passionate about her work, about justice, about exercise, and, of course, about Francis. "The example of Lourdes Maria Cordero Kelly's life is a challenge to me and to all of us to not get lost in the fog of our everyday lives, but to seize every opportunity to serve God, to love, and to live fully the life which is God's greatest gift to us."

Francis starts to cry silently, his shoulders bobbing up and down, and I'm crying too, and Chris is rubbing my back and he's crying, and Tommy sees us both crying and starts to cry. I look around, and everybody is in tears. Even Mr. Cordero, who I expected to be kind of stoic here, has tears streaming down his cheeks. Father Tim says a prayer, and the casket is lowered into the ground. We all get roses and chuck them onto the casket, and then we stagger to the limos.

"Ugh," I say to Chris. "I am so totally exhausted. I can't believe we have to go have the stupid reception thing. I just want to go to sleep."

"No!" Tommy says. "No napping!"

Chris and I laugh, and he hugs me. Despite Tommy's injunction, I sleep all the way back to Francis's house. When we get there, a passel of women are bustling in the kitchen, and casseroles and hors d'oeuvres are emerging from the oven. The house smells like onions and cheese, and I find that I am suddenly ravenous. I head to the kitchen and cut myself a slab of quiche and then pound a mug of coffee. Now I am ready to be social.

The event starts the way these things always do—people congregate in knots in the living room, the dining room, and the kitchen, telling stories about Lourdes and laughing. People approach Francis from time to time to talk to him, and he actually responds to them, which I think is a good sign.

But then I start seeing people walk away from Francis with strange looks on their faces. I decide I should go over and investigate. I get to Francis's side just as Cousin Kieran is saying, ". . . but you know God only gives us what He knows we can handle."

"Gee, Kieran," Francis replies. "You're healthy, your wife is healthy, you've got a beautiful baby girl, your career is in great shape, so I guess God thinks you're pretty much of a pussy, then, doesn't He?"

Kieran stands there with his mouth hanging open. I stand there with my mouth hanging open. There are three or four people in between us who stand there, bite of steaming quiche tottering on the plastic fork halfway to their mouth, unsure if they should stare, say something, or just pretend it didn't happen.

Kieran looks like Francis just sucker-punched him, which of course he did, and he retreats with a mumbled, "Sorry for your loss." Everybody else decides to ignore Francis's outburst now and gossip about it later, but that's just not an option for me, so I head over to him.

"Jesus, Francis, that was horrible!"

"Yeah, well he's horrible. Does he think some kind of half-baked greeting card theology is going to comfort me? Does he think there is any single thing he could say that would make this okay?"

"No, he's just a dumb guy who cares about you and doesn't know any kind of appropriate way to tell you that."

"Yeah, bullshit. He just doesn't want my tragedy to shake his faith."

At this moment our Aunt Mary approaches. She was in the midst of the hen party in the kitchen and missed the outburst that has made Francis radioactive to everybody in this room. I shoot her a look that says, "Not now," but she is oblivious.

"Francis," she says, "I'm so very sorry."

"Thanks, Mary." My eyes are bugging out of my head, cartoon style, as I try to convey to Mary that she needs to quit while she's ahead.

"She was a wonderful woman, you know, she was just too good for us here, God wanted her for His own, so He called her home."

"So you see God as some kind of celestial pimp?" I grab Francis's arm and try to pull him away, but he's raising his voice as I drag him toward the spiral staircase to the basement. "I mean, you're getting on in years, Mary, why do you think God doesn't want you for one of His heavenly bitches?"

I practically shove him down the stairs at this. He has completely lost his mind. We get to the basement, and Francis collapses on the couch. "Francis, what the hell is wrong with you? I mean, I know what the hell is wrong with you, but you can't just go saying stuff like that!"

"Well, they shouldn't say such stupid stuff to me. I hate them all."

"Francis, they're our family."

"You're the one who is always complaining about them. You were right! All these years you were right about all of them!"

"Ugh, Francis, you are insane right now. Just sit here and listen to some music or something. I am going to go upstairs and try to undo the damage."

"Thank you," and now, suddenly, he's crying again. "I love you, you know."

"I know. I love you too."

"I just want her back, I don't want to have to talk to people about why she's gone, I don't want to talk to anybody but my sweet baby, and she's gone, and I hate everybody who's not dead. Except you and your family and Mom and Dad."

"I know, sweetie. Listen, would you like to pray with me?"

"No, thanks. It feels like licking the boot that kicked me." Now I'm the one who's been sucker-punched. I stand there, nonplussed, as Francis goes over to the CDs, grabs something, and puts it on. I find my legs again and remember that I have to go upstairs and do damage control, so I head over to the spiral staircase. As I circle up the steps, I hear crowd noise and the opening bars of Motörhead's "Ace of Spades."

The music is competing with the classical music playing in the living room, and everyone looks at me strangely as I come up the steps. I decide to take advantage of the opportunity to make an announcement.

"Hey, everybody. Francis needs a little time by himself, so please don't go down there, and please don't try to say anything comforting to him. He really can't be comforted right now, and he doesn't seem to be in total control of his mouth. Thanks."

At least an hour past the time when the polite guests have gone home, the "party" finally winds down, I say an incongruous tearful goodbye to Francis to the dulcet strains of "Motörhead" and stagger to the car with Chris and the kids. I know I'll be back tomorrow, and I hope to God Francis has moved off that couch. I slide into the passenger seat and I just start to cry for him, that I can't protect him from this, that he has to hurt so bad. I pray, because I don't know what else to do. "God, please help him. Holy Mother, please watch over my little brother and comfort him." It's not much, but it's all I can do. And now I have to go back to my own house and live my life and try not to worry about Francis, at least until tomorrow.

W̶E ARE AT Francis's house the next two days, and then, as always happens, everybody drifts back to their lives. Even me. As much as I want to take care of Francis, I am just not up to it right now. When I take Mom and Dad to the airport, Dad says to me, "Remember to take care of yourself too, sweetie. Sometimes I'm afraid you put yourself too low on the list."

"Thanks," I say, and as Mom reaches for me, she says, "I'm really very proud of you, dear. I always have been." This doesn't really square with what I have interpreted as more or less constant disapproval, but maybe I've been wrong, or maybe this whole thing has shown Mom that life is too short and she should take it easy on me. I suppose, for that matter, I should take it easy on her.

And so life goes on. I am still calling Francis every day, and we have a standing date for him to come to our house for dinner every Sunday, and I drop by his house after work on Wednesday. Even still, it doesn't feel like enough.

The first few weeks go okay. He's very subdued and pretty much unable to converse when he comes out to our house, but he does seem to appreciate the company. When I go to his house, I always find several crushed-up pizza boxes in the trash, and his hamper is full of laundry. This doesn't make me feel much better, because it's clear that my visits are the only things making him feign normalcy. So if I could just go every day, he might get more normal. But I just can't do it.

Fortunately, or possibly unfortunately, Francis doesn't have to go back to work. Lourdes's parents actually gave them both pretty extravagant life insurance policies for a wedding present, which Chris and I mocked them for and Francis thought was sweet. It turns out to be really sweet, as the house is paid off and he's got enough money to live pretty comfortably for several years or longer. I'm glad that he doesn't have to worry about losing the house or anything, but at the same time, I wish he had a reason to get out of the house other than dinner at my house and the occasional pizza pickup. (He assures me he doesn't always get it delivered, and as messed up as he is, I don't think he'd lie to me.)

Whenever I go to his house, I let myself in, despair at the clutter covering every surface on the first floor, and go down to the basement, where he's parked in front of his enormous TV (which Lourdes never would have allowed, and which he bought online and had delivered) with the sound booming out of all five of the home theater speakers and powered subwoofer behind the couch. (Chris almost literally drooled when Francis described the setup for him one night at dinner, and I had to put my foot down lest Chris start advocating the same thing for our house.) He's not really watching anything—he changes channels incessantly and almost mechanically. Once he flips through some rerun of Joan Rivers on the red carpet, and I say, "Wait, go back, what the hell was that woman wearing?" and he just looks at me blankly. He has no idea what I'm talking about. His eyes were open, and he was looking at the television as long as I was, but the images did not register on his brain.

This goes on, and it's so disturbing that I'm actually relieved if I ever catch him sobbing. "Where is she?" he'll ask me. "Where is she? Why isn't she here? How can she just be gone?" I have no answers for him, so I try to distract him with food.

One month after Lourdes's death, I walk into the house, and I immediately sense something wrong. It takes me a minute to realize what's wrong is that the house is shockingly clean. I don't see any piles of newspapers or magazines or mail on the horizontal surfaces, the rugs appear to have been vacuumed, and there are no dirty dishes sitting in the sink. I run downstairs, expecting to find a newly energized, mentally healthy Francis.

Instead, I find the lights out, the TV on, and Francis parked on the couch, wearing Lourdes's Harvard Medical School sweatshirt, which he always wears and which creeps me out but which he made very clear to me was an off-limits topic of conversation. He's flicking through channels as mindlessly as ever.

"Hey, Francis."

"Hey, Clare. Do you know they never show videos on MTV anymore?"

"Yeah, Francis, they haven't for like ten years."

"So where's the M? I mean, what's the M for?"

"I think it's 'moron.'" I wait, but I get no reaction for this top-notch, off-the-cuff joke. "So, uh, you cleaned, huh? The house looks fantastic!"

"It does? Oh, yeah, Giselle and Teresa did it."

"Um, who the hell are Giselle and Teresa?"

"Oh, yeah, well, I was in this new pizza place—which I am never going back to, because it was a stealth Greek pizza place . . ."

"What?"

"You know, the whole Greek pizza/Italian pizza dichotomy?"

"I really have no idea what you're talking about."

"Basically most of the pizzerias in town are now run by Greeks, and they have this horrible greasy crust, every single one of them, and so you really have to hunt around to find a pizza place run by Italians with that good crust."

"Okay. I'm sorry, but what does this have to do with Giselle and Teresa?"

"Oh, right, so I'm in line over there at Pizza Roma, which is just totally false advertising, since this guy Stavros Drepanos is the owner, but anyway, these guys in front of me in line were talking about how they had their house cleaned by, and I'm quoting here, 'these two sexy Brazilian chicks,' and I thought about how the house just adds to my depression, I mean the filth just reminds me every day of how she's gone, of how she never would have let me let the house get this disgusting. And every day I get up wanting to clean, but I'm just too exhausted, and every single thing up there is something she had or something she touched, and I just can't do it. I have no energy at all. But I do have money, so I called them up, and they did a great job."

"And are they sexy?"

"Oh, I don't even know. They kind of disgust me. Actually all women disgust me. I mean, present company excepted, of course. All I can see is what they lack that she had."

"Um, okay, well, I guess it's good you're not one of those creepy rich guys chasing the maids around."

"Yeah." He hasn't really looked at me this whole time. His eyes have been glued to the tube, even though he's changing channels so fast I can't believe he can actually process what's on the screen at all. "Hey," he says. "Did you see my ad?"

"No. What ad?"

"Here." Still without looking away from the television, he grabs a section of newspaper from the couch next to it and holds it out in my direction. "I circled it."

The paper is open to the classifieds, and I am looking through columns of tiny ads that say, "St. Jude—Thanks for prayers answered. —J.B." Placing these ads is part of the deal if St. Jude helps your hopeless cause. I am hoping that Francis may be thanking St. Jude for the peace that prayer brought him while Lourdes was hospitalized, but no such luck. Halfway down the page is this one, circled:

"St. Jude—Thanks for nothing, you old fraud. —F.K." I have nothing to say. I felt like his hiring the sexy Brazilians was a positive sign—not as much as his actually cleaning the house himself, but he took some steps to improve the state of the house, and that seemed hopeful to me, but this just seems bizarre.

"Uh, this is kind of weird. Is it supposed to be funny?"

"No. I was actually totally serious. I thought people should know that St. Jude can let you down."

"Um, okay."

"I mean, the thing is, I know God is real, Clare, I know it. You know it too. It's not something I ever doubt. So it's not like I was praying to something that doesn't exist, and the universe just didn't care and she died, I know I was talking to something real, and He chose not to help."

"Um, well, yeah, I guess, I mean . . ."

"And Father Tim has been through all this stuff with me about my doubts and about all the language in the Psalms and how Christ himself asked why he'd been forsaken, and how God forgives my doubts, and I just got so angry. I didn't ask for His forgiveness. He should ask for mine! I don't really care what He thinks about my doubts, and if He loves me, He's got a twisted way of showing it. So fuck Him!"

We end up having an uneventful lunch after this, but I am depressed all the way home.

I e-mail Mom and Dad, omitting the obscenities and the reference to his ecstatic experience, which, to my knowledge, he's never told them or anyone but me about, but communicating the gist of his comments. I'm hoping Dad will have three books to recommend that will answer Francis's questions perfectly.

Instead, I get this:

These questions trouble us too. Mom especially has been praying daily, asking God why He's chosen Francis to suffer. I don't believe she's gotten an answer. I too am puzzled, but I see so much suffering in people who don't deserve it down here that I can't believe God is singling Francis out. I suppose my question is simply why there is suffering at all. God has withheld an answer from me, but what I always come to, with, I believe, His guidance, is that it doesn't matter why there is suffering. What matters is how we respond to it. Suffering exists, and God wants us to love each other, so we have to comfort the afflicted. How can we ask God to end suffering if we haven't done everything in our own power to end it? I know I don't have to tell you this, but I do believe that there are many people who question God about suffering who should be questioning themselves about what they are doing about it.

None of which helps Francis right now. But your presence and your love do help him. And remember, he will bounce back—you don't have to lift him. I am sure of this. I love you both. Please tell Francis to answer his e-mail once in a while. I hate to burden you with the reporter's job.

Love, Dad

Another month passes. There are positive developments: (1) Francis starts shaving regularly. (2) The sexy Brazilians keep the house spotless. (3) Francis, on his own and with no prompting from me, goes to the grocery store and buys a bunch of food. It's mostly prepared foods, frozen foods, and dehydrated foods, but at least it's not pizza.

I start hassling Francis on a regular basis to go back to work. The archdiocese has been better than anyone could expect any employer to be about his absence, essentially agreeing to hold his job for him indefinitely. So I call Francis and say things like, "I think you're ready, and I think it would be good for you. You used to get such energy from working with the kids—maybe you could just go back and do the youth group with Father Tim. You don't have to go back to all the administrative stuff."

He usually counters with something like, "I just don't think I can do it. I mean, I'd be a total fraud. I used to really feel it, you know, like I had something to share with them. Now I just feel empty inside."

"Well, I know that Mom would frown on this motivation, but maybe the kids have something to share with you now."

"I dunno. I'll think about it."

We have this conversation in different forms at least three times. Finally I am at his house one Wednesday afternoon, and he is channel-surfing, and I think I'm finally wearing him down.

"Just the youth group. Not the administrative job. Just go hang out with the kids."

"I don't know. Maybe it would be good for me. Maybe if I go through the motions of being faithful, some of my faith will come back."

"And maybe you'll talk to somebody besides me and start to claw your way back to normalcy."

"Honestly, Clare, I have no idea what normalcy is anymore. I don't feel like there is any such thing anymore. But I guess it would be good to have a reason to get out of the house."

Victory! I feel like jumping up and down. I am about to go grab the phone and have him call Father Tim when his finger slips off the remote or something, and he inadvertently pauses on one of the news channels. This is what we hear:

". . . Father Hobson, arraigned today on fourteen counts of sexual assault on a minor. Father Hobson spent the last two years in the New Hampshire diocese after serving in two parishes in the Boston archdiocese."

Francis looks stunned.

"Oh, God, Clare, it's that guy."

"Yeah, Francis, he's been all over the news for the last two weeks."

"Well, I usually just channel-surf. I can't believe it. I can't believe . . . I mean . . . ugh. You work at these retreats, and you know, you hear stuff. He was one of the guys that I heard enough stuff about that I finally went to the Cardinal about it. I mean, that wasn't something I did lightly, you know, I don't just get to walk into his office—there are like three levels I have to go through just to get to his secretary. Anyway, he told me he'd handle it, looked me in the eye and got all serious and was like oh, the safety of our children is our most serious concern, and he'd make sure the guy got help at some program the church runs and that he'd never be a parish priest in Boston again."

"Well, I guess he didn't actually lie . . ."

"He transferred him to New Hampshire! He knew about this! He sent a child rapist to another diocese, and he knew! He knew! Shit!" and he kicks over the coffee table.

I stand there, stunned, and Francis starts to cry. "How could he do it, Clare, how could he do it, those poor kids, oh God, those kids, he could have protected them, he knew. Fourteen kids in two years!"

"Um . . . I'm sorry, Francis."

"You have nothing to be sorry about. It's that evil old man who should be sorry! I can't believe I ever defended him. You know, she used to talk all the time about what an asshole he was, and I was always taking his side, 'he's trying his best, he's old-fashioned but his heart is in the right place'! God! I defended him to her!" And he's gone. He cries for half an hour, occasionally coming up for air to say, "My sweetie, my poor sweetie, why can't I have her back," or, "Those kids, those poor kids, those kids . . ."

Finally I get him calmed down, and I heat up some frozen chicken breast strips and throw them in a tortilla with some cheese for him. He eats it and goes to bed, and I drive back to my house, exhausted.

SUNDAY HE COMES to our house for dinner, and he looks unusually bright and cheerful. He brings wine, which he hasn't done since Lourdes died. As soon as I greet him, he says, "Hey, do you want to see my resignation?"

"Uh, okay . . ." This is what it says:

Cardinal Chapman:

You will forgive me if I don't address you as "Your Eminence," as I believe the title confers a level of respect you are not due. Having seen the news about Father Hobson (about whom I complained to you in 1998, just before you transferred him to New Hampshire), I no longer feel that I can, in good conscience, continue to work for the archdiocese. To talk to children about morality while in the employ of an accessory to child rape would constitute a level of hypocrisy I would be unable to stomach.

If there is any human justice, you will be arrested, convicted, and sentenced to a maximum security facility where you receive horrible

9999999999999999999
6666666666666666666666666

sexual abuse on a regular basis. If there is any divine justice, angels with swords of flame will carve up your body and their demon brethren will drag your soul screaming to hell.

Fortunately for you, it appears that neither justice exists, so I am confident you will enjoy a comfortable old age in a freedom you don't deserve.

I am proud of the work I did at the archdiocese, and I am deeply ashamed of my association with you.

Sincerely,
Francis Kelly

"Jesus, Francis, this is crazy. Angels with swords of flame? You have completely lost your mind! I hope you know you are never sending this."

"Too late. I mailed it yesterday."

"Oh my God, Francis, you didn't."

"Yes, I did. And it felt great!"

"Jesus Christ! You said you wanted demons to drag his soul to hell! You've completely lost your fucking mind!" At this Chris pops his head into the hallway and says, "Hon, every child within five miles can hear you, especially ours, so could you watch the potty mouth?"

"No! I'm sorry, but just read this! He sent this to the Cardinal! The Cardinal! Jesus, Francis, what if you ever wanted a recommendation?"

"Clare, the man recommends child molesters. Anyway, it's not like I have to work."

"Yes you do! You have to work so you can get out of your dark basement and turn off the TV and stop crying all the time and have a goddamn life! Jesus! I can't believe you! You are getting therapy, man, I don't care, I am not ever setting foot in your house again, and you are never coming here again until you get some professional help. I am serious." And here I see Francis and Chris, that quisling, exchange a "here she goes" look, and that makes me determined not to stop, not that I was stopping anyway. "You have gone completely around the bend. People just don't do stuff like this, Francis, they don't write weird religious threats to the frigging Cardinal, I mean the guy gets to vote for the next Pope! I have had it! I can't carry you anymore, Francis, I can't do it, you make it too hard! You have to snap the fuck out of it!"

I storm upstairs and slam my bedroom door, leaving Chris to explain Mommy's little tantrum and her potty mouth to the kids, and hopefully leaving Francis to stew in his own juices for a few minutes.

I lie on my bed in the dark, going over everything I just said and suddenly regretting that I used a metaphor straight out of "He Ain't Heavy, He's My Brother." I have always hated that song, but I especially hate it now, because the person who wrote it obviously never met Francis.

There is a little tap-tap-tap at the door, which is usually what the kids do when I retreat up here. "What?" I bark.

"Um, Clare? Can I come in?" Of course it is not one of my actual children.

"Okay."

"Um, listen, I mean, well, I don't really regret what I sent to the Cardinal, I mean I don't think it's crazy because I think it would be crazy for me to keep working for him, but I know I'm a complete mess, and I can't have you stop coming over, and I can't stop coming over here. You guys are the only humans I ever see who aren't either on a television, cleaning my house, or selling me pizza."

"What about at the grocery store?"

"I use the self-checkout."

"Okay. I think it will help you to talk to somebody. Do you want me to find you someone?"

"Um, I guess so, yeah, if you don't mind. I don't know if any guys in the pizza place will be talking about their sexy Brazilian therapists."

"Well, you never know, but I'll talk to Andie the social worker I work with and see if she knows anybody good for you."

"Okay. Thank you."

"Yeah, well, you're welcome."

"Um, so, um, are we gonna eat? Are you going to emerge, or are you going to sit here in the dark like some pathetic sibling of yours? Do you want me to get the remote control for you?"

I laugh in spite of myself. "Just give me five or ten by myself here. Chris is cooking, so you know he needs all the help he can get. Go see if he'll let you chop or grate something. Or maybe you can just get the kids to abuse you for a while so they don't kill each other."

"Okay."

ANDIE TELLS ME she knows of a great guy who works out of Beth Israel who specializes in bereavement. I'm glad he doesn't work out of Good Sam, because I think that would just give Francis an excuse not to go. I pass his name on to Francis and harass him daily to see if he's made an appointment.

He hasn't by Wednesday when I see him, but when he arrives at my house on Sunday afternoon, he's smiling, holding wine, and wearing real pants. Not sweatpants, not even jeans, but some nice pair of pants that Lourdes probably bought for him or coached him on. He's wearing a similarly stylish shirt, and it's a tremendous relief to see him in something other than Lourdes's med school sweatshirt.

I have drawn dinner prep duty this time, and Francis stands in the kitchen with me. It's cold, and it's getting dark early, but Chris is outside in sweats tossing a Nerf football with the kids and doing fantastic pratfalls whenever they grab him. I have a sad flashback to sitting at the table with big glasses of wine watching Francis cavort with the kids while Lourdes told me they were trying to conceive.

I suddenly miss her terribly. She made me happy, and she made Francis happy, and my life was easier when I didn't have to worry about him so much. Their kids will never get to maul him in this backyard, and that part seems especially cruel. God knows Francis couldn't take care of a child in his condition, but it just feels wrong that nobody's carrying her DNA, nobody is going to grow up to look like her, nobody will cock their head like her, or be ambitious like her, or remind us of her at all. It's a terrible loss to us, but to the rest of the world too. She feels completely gone to me, and I'm angry at how unfair it is, and I feel lucky that this feeling only comes in brief flashes. If Francis feels this way and worse all the time, I can hardly blame him for not getting off the couch and for never going to mass or praying anymore.

"Hello? I said John was able to squeeze me in right away! I went to therapy!" I'm back, and Francis appears to be talking to me.

"Uh, wow, hey that's great! How did you like the guy?"

"He seems pretty nice. He didn't yell at me for sitting on the couch all the time, and he didn't call me a loser or anything. He said, 'We always call something like this a devastating loss, so I'm not at all surprised that you're devastated.' "

"Well, that's good," I say, but I'm thinking this stupid quack was supposed to help me kick Francis's ass, not tell him that his life in Plato's cave was somehow normal.

"And I'm wearing my happy clothes. I told him about how I hated the look of the house and about the sexy Brazilians, and he asked me how I felt about dressing in sweats all the time . . ." Okay, maybe he's not such a quack after all. "So he said maybe if I went through the motions of dressing like I did when I was happy, it might help me feel less screwed up."

"Well, you look better than you have since she died. How's it working?"

"I don't know. I mean, I am aware that I look better, but I don't really care about that. I still feel completely empty inside."

Careful to put down my knife, I hug him. "You're important to me. I know it's not enough, but it is something. And the kids love you. Why don't you go let them tackle you or something?"

"But it's cold."

"Just go through the motions, Francis. It might make you happy for a minute."

"Okay. But I'm wearing my good pants. I don't want to ruin my happy clothes."

"I'm sure you have other pants. You can buy yourself another pair tomorrow. It'll get you out of the house."

"Okay, okay."

So Francis bundles up, and suddenly a tall, gangly Yeti interrupts the football game, and the kids gamely defend their poor father by tackling and pummeling the snow beast relentlessly.

THREE MORE LONG months pass. I wish I could say that the therapy helps tremendously, but the obvious gains stop with Francis wearing real clothes every day. He gets up every day, showers, shaves, puts on real clothes, and parks himself in front of the television for at least twelve hours. He is no longer doing anything as crazy as telling the Cardinal that he wants demons to drag his soul to hell, though four more pedophile priests that Cardinal Chapman covered for are arrested during this time, and I start thinking maybe Francis was prophetic rather than crazy. I suppose there's always been an incredibly thin line there.

So worrying about Francis becomes background noise in my life, and I always have the strangest sensation of jumping tracks whenever I see him—my regular life is hectic and involves a lot of running around, and time seems to be on permanent fast-forward. I find an Arthur book I got out of the library to read to Tommy, and I can't understand how it could be a month overdue when we just finished it the other night. I actually go and ask Tommy, and he looks at me like I'm nuts and says, "Mommy! We read that like a year ago!"

And yet, when I see Francis, it's like stepping into molasses. It's like he's able to stop time in his basement, and nothing much changes down there for a really long time. It's annoying, and I wish it would stop, but in a weird way it makes things easier. As long as Francis is stuck in the molasses, I know he's not getting better, but he's also not getting worse. I can stop worrying about him for long stretches and actually pay close attention to my children and start to open up to my patients a little more. Being caring and completely present with the dying is an important part of my job, and I feel like worrying about Francis was stopping me from doing this well. I still got tearful hugs and thanks from the families, but I had been feeling like a fraud.

I get a new patient, a woman about Lourdes's age dying of breast cancer who lives near Francis, so I try to arrange my visits there so I can have lunch with Francis again. It is often a pretty tough transition. The breast cancer patient, whose name is Samantha, is tall, blond, and nothing like Lourdes, except that she is driven professionally, some kind of big-shot executive at Fidelity, and she has a husband who looks just as frightened and lost as Francis. She also has a six-year-old son. Usually he's at school when I make my visits, but sometimes I don't get over there until two, and then Jeff brings little Conor home, and he runs up to his ever-yellowing mother and hugs her, and I have to busy myself with stuff in my bag in order to wall this off from the part of me that wants to bawl. Sometimes when Jeff is out of the room, Samantha says to me, "I worry about Jeff—he's great with Conor, but he doesn't even know the kid's shoe size. How is he going to do this?"

"He'll do it because he has to," I say, which I believe to be true, but I'm still glad I won't be here to watch it because it will probably be messy. When I get into my car to drive over to Francis's house, I wish again that he and Lourdes had successfully reproduced. Because then Francis would have something he had to do, a focus for his energy, something to do besides watch television, some way out of the molasses.

And then, one day, he does get a focus for his energy, and it only worries and disturbs me.

I arrive at his house at noon, let myself in, and head down to the basement. The shade is open on the tiny window at the top of the wall, so he's watching TV in a mild gloom instead of total darkness. Francis is wearing a nice gray sweater and jeans that look like they are nearly worn out, which indicates that they are not his regular jeans but, rather, Fashion Jeans that he has probably squandered a silly amount of his insurance payoff on.

"Hey! New jeans!"

"Yeah." Click. Click. This is the most unnerving part of talking to Francis in this basement—he just never stops changing channels. "I ordered them online. I thought maybe if I had some new happy clothes it would help me find some new happiness."

"How's that working out?"

"Well, I still feel like I've been kicked in the stomach, but I did pull the shade."

"I noticed. Come on, let's get out of here."

"Okay." He turns off the television and slips on some obviously expensive black happy shoes, and we head off to the Hong Kong Garden, about three trash-strewn blocks from his house.

We sit in a booth with threadbare green upholstery patched with green electrical tape beneath a red sign with golden characters on it and have an uneventful lunch. I talk about Alvin, the pain-in-the-ass old guy who is always yelling at me that I'm an evil drug pusher, that I'm trying to get him hooked on drugs, that it's people like me who are ruining this country. I taught his wife to smash his oxycodone into some applesauce, since he refuses to take a pill and is making everyone else suffer because of his pain.

Francis nods, eats his General Tso's chicken, and doesn't say much. What can he say? He doesn't have anything to add to a conversation—he never even stays on one channel long enough to absorb anything he could talk about, except, strangely, hockey, which is just actively uninteresting to me.

This depresses me, and I have to be in Norwood by two, so I drain the remnants of my jasmine tea and signal for the check. I grab it, and Francis says, "Come on, now. You have to let me pick this up." I know what his bank account looks like, so I don't argue.

I am getting ready to get up when a young woman starts walking toward our table. Her hair is badly dyed blond and up in high pigtails. She has on too much mascara and lipstick. She is wearing worn-out-looking jeans that are not quite as artfully distressed as Francis's jeans, which signals thrift store rather than high fashion. I can't quite figure out how they are staying up and covering everything pants need to cover when they are riding so very low below her hips. She's wearing a black tank top (in December!) with red bra straps peeking out, and on her left arm is a large tattoo that appears to be Our Lady of Guadalupe.

"Francis?" she says.

"Um, yes? Oh my God, Angie?"

"Yes!"

"Wow, it's great to see you! Angie, you remember my sister, Clare, she came to the youth group to talk about death once. Clare, you remember Angie, she busted your chops with hard questions!"

"Uhh . . . well, that was a long time ago." And anyway, I want to protest, that room was full of awkward, pimply teens, visibly uncomfortable in their own skins. Who is this clear-skinned young woman with the scandalously hot body? And how is it that you are young and hot, and I am some suburban matron? I have Dead Kennedys albums older than you! I say none of this. Instead, I say, "Well, I really have to run . . ."

And Francis, instead of saying, it's great to see you, hope you're doing well, says, "Well, Clare has to go back to work, but I no longer have those constraints. Do you want to have some jasmine tea and catch up for a few minutes?"

At this, Angie's face lights up. "Sure! I'd love that! I was just gonna get some veggie lo mein and go back to my disgusting apartment!"

I say goodbye to both of them and drive to Norwood, where a fifty-year-old woman named Carla is dying from an inoperable brain tumor. Her apartment is dark and stuffy, and she is always watching soaps with the sound turned down and the captions on. Every time I see her, she laments the affair (hers) that led to her divorce, and the fact that her eighteen-year-old son won't forgive her. Her sister, Vicky, bustles and cries. I try my best not to show it, but I always feel like I'm suffocating at Carla's house—like the combination of the hot air, the soaps, Carla's regret, and Vicky's slow grief conspire to stop me from breathing. Even when it's freezing out, I stand outside my car for five minutes after leaving Carla's place before I can stand to get into another enclosed space.

After dinner that evening, I put the kids to bed, and the phone rings. Chris yells out, "Hon, it's Francis!"

I take a deep breath. He almost never calls unless he's feeling particularly screwed up, and I steel myself for talking him through a crying jag. I'm so tired of this, and I can hear hardness in my voice when I pick up the phone. "Hello?"

"Clare!" And his voice is brighter than I've heard it since before that horrible day when he called me after Lourdes collapsed.

"Hey, are the kids in bed, I didn't pull you away from the kids, did I, because I can call back if you need a few minutes." And he's talking a mile a minute. It's like my brother is back, and that basement-dwelling mole man he's become has just melted away.

"No, Francis, they're asleep. What's going on?"

"Oh my God, I just had the greatest afternoon. I sat there with Angie until five o'clock, we talked about everything, I mean I told her my story, and we talked a lot about God and everything. It was weird, you know, she still goes to mass."

"Um, good for her. I wish you'd go back."

"I wish I wanted to. I don't know, maybe I will, I mean, well, anyway, she lives just down the street from me, and she plays in a band, and she works in a used record store, but she is just, I mean, she was always this incredibly interesting kid, you know, much more thoughtful than the average teen, and she still is, I mean she has this fantastic mind."

Now, it's been several years, but I recognize this conversation. This is the "I just met the best girl" conversation. I don't know exactly how to feel. On the one hand, it is really wonderful to hear Francis excited about something. He sounds alive for the first time since Lourdes's death. On the other hand, Angie was one of his youth group charges, and she must be at least ten years younger than him, and so this huge crush on her is pathetic and vaguely creepy.

"Um, Francis, you know you can't date this girl."

"What are you talking about? I'm a single man!"

"Francis, she's, what, twelve years younger than you? It's just gross—and she probably has some kind of boyfriend who's a drummer or something who is her own proper age, and finally, this is the kind of girl you always used to date before Lourdes. Do you remember all those punk rock girls?"

"Yes, but they weren't as smart as Angie is. And they always got freaked out about my going to church, and Angie still goes to mass!"

"Well, Francis, I mean, um, this, it's just weird, I mean, there's the whole weird power dynamic thing, I mean she probably has this trust in you because of the whole youth group thing, and it just feels icky to me."

"Clare, she's an adult! It's not like she's fifteen or something!"

"But she was fifteen when you were already an adult! Her having some kind of *To Sir, with Love* crush on you is a crappy foundation for a relationship. And, anyway, chasing younger women—"

"I'm not chasing her, Clare. I just had tea and pot stickers with her. I'm not going to stalk her or anything, I mean, I know it's a long shot, it's not like something that's really going to happen, but I feel—I mean, we hugged goodbye, and it was like I was back from the dead or something. It was almost electric—like she's this battery of life energy, and she jump-started me."

"Are you sure it wasn't just your libido she jump-started?"

"Yes! I mean, yeah, that too, but it wasn't just that."

"I don't know. I'm glad to hear you like this—I think it's great, I really do. But I just worry that you are going to get hurt and, I'm sorry, embarrassed, and I'm worried about you getting off the mat the next time you get knocked down."

"Okay. I'm getting angry at you, Clare, and I love you too much to say what I am thinking right now, so I am going to hang up the phone." And he hangs up on me! Francis! Hangs up on *me!*

I walk to the living room to find Chris. He's sitting in the big leather chair reading a magazine, and the wimpy adult radio station we always listen to (yes, even me, and yes, I do like Elvis Costello's recent work and, God help me, even Van Morrison) is playing softly through the speakers.

"Francis just hung up on me!"

Chris looks up. "Wow, that's weird. I thought you were the one who got exasperated in that relationship."

"So did I! Well, listen to this—we ran into this girl at the Chinese restaurant today who used to be in Francis's youth group, and now she's this sexy, I don't know, maybe twenty-two-year-old, and he's got this big crush on her!"

Chris looks at me blankly. There is only one right way for him to react here, and he's already dangerously down the wrong path. "Um, yeah?" He's trying, which should earn him some points, but I can tell it won't.

"Yeah! So my thirty-five-year-old brother has this big crush on somebody twelve years younger than him! It's pathetic, and he's going to get his heart broken, and make a fool of himself, and did I mention that it's kind of creepy?"

"Um, so, I mean, and I'm sorry here, I'm not trying to be a smart-ass, but isn't he kind of pathetic already? Let's say Lolita does break his heart—is he going to be any worse off than he is now? *Could* he be any worse off than he is now?"

Wrong answer! "Ugggh! I knew you wouldn't understand!" And I storm off.

I chew on this for two days or so before I decide that I guess Chris is right as far as the pathetic part goes. If he's out of the house buying used records and shopping in thrift stores and generally pretending to be a decade younger, at least he's out of the house doing something, and he's connecting to something that was important to him in a previous life. And, from a completely selfish point of view, this stuff is much more interesting to me than his esoteric hockey knowledge. Hopefully this will get him to stop talking about the Bruins' fourth line, whatever the hell that is.

I call Francis on Friday. I haven't talked to him since he hung up on me, and I'm surprised to find that I miss him.

"Hello?"

"Hey, Francis. Are you still mad at me?"

"Oh no, Clare, of course not. I know that this concern is just a manifestation of your love for me, and so in that respect it's kind of touching."

"Uh, well, good. Are you still coming to dinner on Sunday?"

"Oh, of course."

"Good," I say, and I exhale, realizing I've been holding my breath ever since he hung up on me.

There is silence for a moment, and then he says, "Um, can I ask you a favor?"

Here it comes. It's always something, or at least it has been since Lourdes died.

"Well, you can always ask," I say in my bitch voice.

"Okay. I need you to come out with me next Tuesday. Chris can come too, if you want to get a baby-sitter. I'll even pay! The only thing is that it's in Cambridge and it's kind of late."

"Well, what is it?"

"Um . . . well, there's this band I want to go see at GTO's."

"Aw, Francis, is this Angie's band?"

"Well, yeah."

"Oh, Francis, I'm thirty-seven years old! I cannot be one of the three people seeing some band at GTO's on a Tuesday night at midnight. And then I'll be exhausted the next day and my clothes and my hair will reek of smoke . . ."

"No—Cambridge has a smoking ban! Come on, she called me and asked me to go, I mean, this is not me stalking her, she invited me. And I can't be the only person over thirty in the club—I just can't, you're right about that part, I mean it would feel too pathetic."

"So I have to feel pathetic with you?"

"Bring Chris! We'll all be pathetic together!"

"Ugh. All right, I'll talk to Chris. You know, if you weren't my brother, and insane with grief, I wouldn't even consider this."

"And if you weren't my sister, I'd still love you, because you are a beautiful person." Goddammit. If I thought he had a manipulative bone in his body, I might really resent how good he just made me feel. I know before I hang up the phone that I'm going to go, because how else am I going to feel like St. Clare? I sign off with some feigned grumpiness about how I have to ask Chris, and there's no way for us to get a baby-sitter on this kind of notice, does he know that these fourteen-year-old girls run the suburbs, maybe we can ask Chris's mom, but she's been so helpful in the last few months that I feel bad asking her again.

But of course I do ask her, and of course she says yes, because she is kind of saintly herself. So Tuesday night rolls around. Francis assures us that there is no way Angie's band—which, by the way, is called Mary's Cherry—is starting before midnight. This means that we are able to put the kids to bed ourselves, and that all Chris's mom has to do is sit here. It also means that we are going to an event that starts two hours later than we usually go to bed. I brew us a pot of coffee at nine o'clock and start getting grumpy about how tired I'm going to be tomorrow, and how the whole rest of this week is basically shot.

And then there is the question of what to wear. I decide as long as we are being pathetic, I am going to try to be somewhat cool, which, let's face it, I simply haven't been at all since the kids were born. I find my black boots, and I cram my enormous butt into the rattiest jeans I have. I put on a black bra and dig through the "paint-ing clothes" pile and find a Ramones shirt. Pretty much everybody respects the Ramones these days, so I figure it's safe, though it does date to the Richie Ramone era, and he has been essentially written out of the history of the band. I am thirty-seven years old, and I stand in the doorway of my closet for a full five minutes trying to de-cide whether having the shirt with "Richie" on it makes me cooler than all the kids with their shirts that say "Tommy." I suppose I can't really berate Francis for being pathetic anymore. I put on too much mascara, and I look at myself. I am afraid I look like somebody's mom trying to be cool, which is I suppose what I am.

Chris, to his credit, doesn't even try to be cool. He's wearing his standard casual wear: clean, neat jeans from the Gap, a red polo shirt from the Gap, and pristine white New Balance sneakers. His stomach pushes the polo shirt out in a way that announces his age as much as my butt announces mine. I wince at his outfit and feel sort of embarrassed that this is as cool as Chris can be. His musical experiences consist of seeing bands like Dire Straits and John Mellencamp in outdoor arenas every summer, so his getup is en-tirely appropriate to his concert-going experiences.

Clearly the worst part of all this is that it makes me hate myself: for being middle-aged and fat, for caring about being cool like I'm a teenager, for letting Francis take me out of my comfort zone.

Chris helps somewhat, though. When he sees me, he goes, "Ooo, punk rock chick! You are totally hot!" His assessment contrasts so completely with what I saw in the mirror that I think he must be lying or delirious with love. He grabs me and kisses me. It helps take some of the sting out of this evening.

We drive to Cambridge and meet Francis on the street outside GTO's. He, of course, looks much younger than he is, and he also still has the physique and the wardrobe to carry off the rock club look pretty convincingly. He's wearing black jeans that have faded to a dark gray, and an army surplus jacket. Chris and I have our L.L. Bean parkas over our short-sleeved shirts. Ugh.

Francis is obviously colder than we are, as he's hopping up and down on the sidewalk when we arrive. This makes me feel no better about showing up in L.L. Bean. He opens the door and pays for all three of us. He gets asked for ID and smiles broadly as he hands his over.

The bouncer, a giant of a man who can't be more than twenty-two, does not ask me for identification. He also says, "Hey! You got a kid in one of the bands?"

So not only have I failed completely at looking cool, I also have succeeded at looking old enough to have a kid in his twenties. I decide to go with it, as it may be the only way to get any respect around here.

"Yes, my little Angela goes on next. She plays guitar!" I play this up to the height of dorkiness.

The bouncer looks genuinely touched. "You know, that is so great. So many parents just disapprove of their kids, you know. I think it's great that you came out to support her. She is really great, by the way, really talented. I think she's gonna be big. And she's really hot"—and here he glances at Chris somewhat fearfully, which I love—"I mean, no offense or anything, she's just a very attractive young lady."

"I hear you," Chris says. "She takes after her mom."

"See, now my old man . . ." I flee and let Chris hear the rest of the bouncer's life story.

GTO's is much the same as I remember it, except much less smoky. I'm sure it's going to mean that my eyes won't sting and my hair and clothes won't reek, but it somehow feels much less rock and roll. The music takes place to my right, the bar is an island in the middle, and there's a room with a pool table and a jukebox in the other room. A TV is tuned to ESPN. "Hey," Francis says, "did the Bruins win?" and he wanders over toward the television.

There are maybe twelve people here, which is actually nine more than I expected to see. Angie is onstage tuning her guitar. Her hair is down and her tank top is white, but otherwise she looks almost exactly the same as when we saw her in the restaurant. She is surrounded by another guitarist, a bassist, and a drummer, all of whom are men her age, tattooed, muscular, and exactly the kind of guys I pictured being her boyfriend. My money's on the drummer.

I get beers for me and Chris and motion to him at the door so that he will have an excuse to leave the bouncer. I hope Francis has not sneaked around behind me and parked himself in front of the soundboard while my back was turned, but, of course, there he is. Angie sees him when she checks her mike, and she says, "Hey. Thanks for comin' out," in a kind of flat way. I suppose this could be just her being a cool rock and roller, but I like to think it's because she's not really all that glad to see him.

Chris reaches me and I hand him his beer. "That guy is really interesting! He was an emancipated minor! He hasn't talked to his parents in six years—apparently there was some drug abuse, or dealing, or something. He doesn't really like to talk about it. He goes to BU on a football scholarship. I told him we might come out to a game sometime."

I have nothing to say to this. My brother is making an ass of himself, and my husband is adopting the bouncer.

I take a long pull on my beer and turn my attention to the stage. The band appears to be all tuned up and ready to play, but they are hesitating. All twelve patrons come over to the music area, which makes this look somewhat less pathetic, but I am bracing for a very painful performance here—bands are rarely at their best when they're playing to the low double digits.

"All right," Angie says. "Thanks for coming out, we're Mary's

Cherry." They kick into their opening number, and it sounds fine—
they are doing the retro-1970s Kiss/Alice Cooper/Thin Lizzy thing,
which I like fine. There is an immediate problem, though—this
band has a hideous talent imbalance. Angie, out front, is fantastic. I
can't really hear her guitar in the sloppy mix, but she looks great
playing it, and her singing voice is low and, I suppose, sexy. More
than that, though, she just has a fantastic presence onstage. She is
playing her heart out for twelve people, jumping around the stage,
yowling into the mike and sweating profusely. I look over at Chris
and Francis, and then at the five other guys in the crowd, and they
all wear identical expressions of awe. It will not surprise me if any
or all of them start drooling. I hit Chris, because this annoys me,
and he looks kind of sheepish and tries valiantly for the rest of the
set to keep that "O Sweet Jesus I Must Have Her" expression off his
face.

So if Angie has star quality, the others clearly don't. They are no
fun to watch, and they just can't provide steady enough music to
back her up. The drummer and bassist lose each other noticeably
during three different songs, and the bassist and guitarist trade
annoyed looks throughout the set, whenever the guitarist is not
putting a hand to his ear and raising his thumb in an effort to get the
sound guy to bury the rest of the band with his guitar sound. This
band is a mess.

Finally they finish, and I grab Chris and say to Francis, "Listen,
we've got to go, I've gotta work in the morning. What are you
doing?"

He looks completely stunned. "Um . . . I guess . . . I guess . . .
maybe I'm gonna hang out for a few. You know, wish Angie well,
that kind of thing."

"Okay, Francis," and I am about to say something about how he
shouldn't be too disappointed when she locks lips with the drummer, and how he should just go home and go to bed before he gets

his feelings hurt, when she comes bounding up to him, beaming, and says, "Hey! How did we sound! What did you think of the set?"

"You were great!" Francis says, which is not a lie if he's using the singular "you." Chris and I leave, and it's so freezing outside that I am glad I have my L.L. Bean parka. Chris drives, and I fall asleep on the way home.

*T*HE NEXT DAY is Wednesday, and I sleepwalk through all of my visits despite the giant travel mug of coffee that I refill two or three times during the day. I get to Francis's house, and I'm seriously thinking about asking him if I can crash on his couch for a few minutes rather than having lunch.

When I get to the house, I hear the familiar sound of the Ramones' *Too Tough to Die* booming from the basement. This appears to mean that Francis is not watching television. Sure enough, when I get down to the basement, the TV is off, the stereo is blasting, and Francis is reading *Spin*. It's like he's sixteen again.

"Hey!" I yell, and Francis, smiling, turns the music down.

"Hey," he says. "What do you know about the White Stripes?"

"Nothing," I say. "Never heard of them."

"Apparently they are the future of rock and roll, or the salvation of rock and roll."

"Oh." I am about to ask some snide thing about whether Angie likes them, but I manage to bite my tongue.

"And no, Angie did not mention the White Stripes. I just went out this morning and bought every music magazine I could find, and every single one of them mentions them at least twice."

"You actually left the house to buy magazines? That's great!"

"Yeah, and then I stopped off in the coffee shop and drank lots of coffee and read!"

"Wow, that's good!"

"Yeah. So before you ask, I told her that she was really good, and she should definitely tell me when they are playing again, and then she had to load her equipment out, and she went home with the drummer and did not stay at the bar with me until closing time. But she did say she was going to call me."

"The drummer. I knew it. Did she boyfriend you?"

"What?"

"You know, boyfriend you? Did she ever say the words 'my boyfriend'?"

"Um, no, I don't think so. Why?"

Damn. I asked because I was sure she had boyfriended him, and then I could give him that evidence that he should give up, that she'd sent him the coded message that she wasn't interested. But she didn't boyfriend him. This means either that she is kind of interested in him, or keeping her options open, or else she thinks of Francis as too old to be a potential boyfriend and therefore didn't feel the need to boyfriend him.

"I don't know. I was just curious."

We trek over to the Hong Kong Garden and, fortunately, our lunch is uninterrupted by hot former youths. Francis spreads his music magazines out on the ratty Formica table and totally dominates the conversation. He goes through a list of CDs he wants to buy, and occasionally asks me a question I am unable to answer: "What's emo?" "Who is Andrew W.K.?" I have no idea. Apparently the CD reviews are now using styles and artists I have never heard of as points of reference. I am so very very old. I get embarrassed remembering my club gear—I guess trying to dress for 1984 in 2003 pretty well sums me up.

And what about Francis? He's thirty-five, and he's attacking music magazines with the passion of a sixteen-year-old or one of those scary middle-aged guys who own used record stores, are married only to their music collections, and pine after their tattooed, patchouli-smelling clerks. Actually, at this point, I suppose that's very close to what Francis is. And he's happy, or at least much happier than he's been in months, and I certainly can't begrudge him that—but I want my old brother back. I suppose he probably does too, but apparently that's not an option.

Another week passes. Francis comes over to dinner and alternately entertains and tortures us with his new CD purchases. On Wednesday, I head over to Francis's house for what looks like it might be my last lunch with him for a while, since Samantha, my breast cancer patient, is getting foggier every time I visit due to the toxins building up in her blood due to her failed liver due to metastases from her breast cancer. Her extended family is gathering, she's written a hundred-page autobiography for Conor, and she will soon go wherever the dead go, and then neither I nor anyone else will ever see her again.

When I get to the house, I hear strange noises coming from the basement, and I can feel the vibrations coming through my feet. I call to Francis, but he doesn't answer, so I head down and am greeted with something I did not expect to see: Francis is standing in the basement, and both the TV and the stereo are turned off. He is plucking, apparently at random, strings on a cherry red bass, which is hooked up to a rather gigantic Marshall amp.

"Hey!" he says when he finally sees me. "How are you?"

"Um, I'm fine. What . . . I mean, I know what you're doing, but what are you doing?"

"I'm learning the bass!"

"Okay . . . and why? Wait. Oh no. Please please don't tell me that Angie's band needs a bassist."

"No, they actually need a new guitarist. Apparently that guy was jealous of her onstage mojo."

"Well, he also couldn't play, but then neither could any of the rest

of them except Angie and possibly her boyfriend the drummer."
For some reason I feel a real responsibility to keep Francis somewhat grounded in reality.

"Agh, he's not her boyfriend. They're just roommates!"

"Did she tell you that?"

"No. I mean, I haven't talked to her much in the last two weeks. She's always busy with band stuff or work, but she's never once referred to him as her boyfriend, so just because they cohabitate doesn't mean they're an item."

"Yes it does, but whatever. So if you're not joining Angie's band, why are you learning the bass?"

"I think it's the easiest thing to learn. It's the instrument they always give to the one who can't play. Sid Vicious played bass! He could never play at all, and he played bass! When they wanted Tina Weymouth in Talking Heads and she couldn't play anything, they gave her a bass!"

"Well, okay, I suppose, but what's the goal here? Are you starting a band?"

"Naah. I don't really have anything to say: Boo-hoo my wife is dead, I have a crush on a twenty-two-year-old, and I find that I really like hockey."

"Bands have built entire careers on less than that. You've already got two more ideas than AC/DC ever had."

"Maybe, but I just—I don't want to write songs. I just want to join a band. So I figure the bass is the way to go."

"Why do you think anybody's going to want you to be their bassist?"

"Because nobody wants to play bass! It's not a glamour instrument! Everybody wants to be the guitarist or the singer! So there have to be tons of bands forming that need bassists! Remember that guy in Cincinnati—Karl something? He was in like every band that ever played at the Jockey Club!"

I remember the guy—Francis is exaggerating, but it is true that he did play bass in at least three bands simultaneously. I am sure I saw him open for himself more than once.

"But, I mean, Francis, you're . . . you're . . . you're not really going to add much to the image of most of these bands. I mean, Sid Vicious was a badass, and Tina Weymouth was sleeping with the drummer. I don't think you're bringing anything like that to the table. I mean, you're—"

"I know, Clare, I know. But I still think somebody out there wants to play punk rock and needs a bassist."

"Well, I think you might land a gig in a band doing Cure and Squeeze covers at class reunions and things." That came out meaner than I wanted it to, and he gives me that "you are an awful person" look, and I feel bad for hurting his feelings. But it's for his own good—I think he's setting himself up for yet another fall: now he's chasing his Dee Dee Ramone dream as well as Angie, and these are dreams for younger men. I want to be able to say I told him so. I don't really know why. "Look, Francis, I don't mean . . . I just mean, you know, most twenty-two-year-olds starting bands don't want a thirty-five-year-old bassist."

Now he looks at me with a kind of pity—it's a look that says, "I feel really bad that you are so wrong."

"Well," he says, "I guess we'll see. Here, listen, I've been working on 'Ace of Spades.' " And he proceeds to attempt to pick out the bass line to Motörhead's speed-metal classic at about one-tenth the speed that Lemmy plays it, missing about every third note.

"Um, well, I guess it's coming along. Come on, I'm hungry."

At lunch, after unsuccessfully telling him that he should really learn how to play the bass before he does this, I give in and help Francis write his "Bassist Seeks Band" ad. We look at the *Boston Phoenix* classifieds to get the format down. Apparently you have to list all the bands you like and any experience you have, so I come up with this:

"No experience, no talent, no problem: budding Dee Dee seeks Joey."

"Jeez, you can't really say I have no talent. The paper doesn't come out for another week! I'll be at least as good as Dee Dee by then. I do like the Dee Dee seeks Joey part, though."

"I don't know, Francis, it sounds kind of like a gay personal ad. And anyway, you need a Johnny too, and a Tommy, Richie, or Marky."

"We don't speak of Richie," he says with a laugh. "Okay, how about this: Sober Dee Dee—that's important, I don't want anybody to think I'm a junkie, or they'll never call—seeks Joey, Johnny, and Tommy, but will take Marky or even Richie."

"Well, I don't know if your average twenty-two-year-old is going to get that, Francis."

"Yeah, but if they don't get it, I don't want to be in the band! This will weed out the guys who think Blink-182 is the first punk band."

"Who the hell is Blink-182?"

"They did that song at the end of the first *Charlie's Angels* movie? Anyway, it's not important. This should get people who are into the old school."

"Okay, but if you're calling yourself Dee Dee, you have to learn to play fast, even if you can't really play."

"I know! Jeez!"

"All right, all right, I'm just trying to help!"

Lunch ends, and it's back to work for me, back to trying to play "Blitzkrieg Bop" at faster than ballad speed for Francis.

Francis's ad runs in the *Phoenix* the following week. He comes over for dinner three days later, and makes us listen to the White Stripes again.

"Play the one about first grade, and then put something else on, will you?" I yell from the kitchen.

"Come on! This is such a great record!"

"It's fine, but I'm just a little tired of it. What else do you have?"

"How about the Darkness? They sound like Whitesnake!"

"Is that a good thing? You hate Whitesnake!"

"Yeah, but I think enough time has passed that they're kind of cool in a retro-terrible way."

"Whatever. So how many responses have you gotten to your ad?"

"Um . . . Well, it's been a little slow."

"So, how many?"

"Um . . ."

"Five?" Silence. "Two?" Silence.

"Okay, none. Zero. Nobody."

"Aw, jeez, I'm sorry," I say, hoping I can keep the joy out of my voice. Maybe now Francis will stick to obsessive CD buying, like a normal thirty-five-year-old music geek. "Well, maybe it's a sign. I mean, maybe this band thing isn't meant to be."

"I guess I don't believe in signs anymore. And I know you're worried about me making a total ass of myself with the bass, with Angie, and everything. But the thing is that the stakes are really low here."

"I don't know—it seems like they're pretty high."

"Naah. See, I have finally accepted the fact that Lourdes isn't coming back. But that must mean that this isn't my real life. So if it's not my real life, I can do anything! Nothing matters, because I'm not living my real life!"

"But . . . um . . . it is your real life."

"Well, of course it is, I mean I'm not completely insane, but I just don't feel like any of this matters very much."

"So you're not going to be devastated if it doesn't work out?"

"Oh it's going to work out," he says, sounding completely convinced. "I have a trump card."

"Oh yeah? What? Your awesome bass talent?"

"Hey, I can play the first Ramones album all the way through! And now I'm working on 'Bad Brain' for an audition piece! But anyway, no, it's not that. You'll see. I'll keep it a surprise."

I AM, IN FACT, surprised, when I drop by Francis's house the following week, because I am greeted at the door by a bare-chested, sweaty, gorgeous, dark-complected young man with beautiful eyes and even more beautiful muscles. I lose my power to speak, both because I am surprised to find anybody but Francis here and because this guy has plaster dust kind of clinging to the sweat drops that are running down . . .

"Uh . . ." I say. "Uh . . ."

"Francis?" he says helpfully.

"Yeah."

"Upstairs. Francis!"

Francis's voice comes from upstairs—upstairs!—and says, "Yeah, João?"

"Somebody here!" and João disappears downstairs.

"Thanks!"

And he descends, dressed in his happy clothes. "Hey! Ready to go?"

"Um, yeah, what's going on?"

"I'm playing my trump card."

"You're having an affair with a sexy Brazilian?"

"Is he sexy?"

"Oh my God."

"Huh? No, João is Teresa's cousin, and he's doing some carpentry work for me."

"In the basement?"

"Yeah. I moved the stereo up here. The TV is still down there—I find I don't really watch it much these days anyway."

I press Francis all through lunch about what his trump card is and what's happening in the basement, but all he'll tell me is that I should wait for his ad in this week's *Phoenix*.

I grab the *Phoenix* when it comes out, and I spot Francis's ad immediately. He's tightened it up considerably, but the essential information is all there: "Bassist with practice space, van, seeks band." His trump card is, of course, his bank account. His inability to play the bass and his age suddenly evaporate as factors in any band's decision. When I dated guys in bands in college (yes, Francis was not the only one who pursued dates that were horribly wrong for him), they were always getting kicked out of practice spaces they couldn't afford and cramming all their equipment into fifteen-year-old vans on life support. Francis has a basement that I'm guessing João was soundproofing and, if I know him, a brand-new van. I wonder if he traded in the Volvo—that would certainly send Lourdes spinning in her grave.

When Francis comes over on Sunday, he's grinning broadly. "Just guess, Clare. Just guess how many calls."

"I don't know—fifteen."

"One hundred. One hundred. I am pretty sure that every band in the Greater Boston Area called me."

"You must have pissed off a lot of bassists."

I promise to help Francis sort through the replies, and so after dinner, Chris puts the kids to bed, and Francis and I look at his notes. We throw out every band that mentions Rush, which proves to be a surprisingly high number—the sensibility is all wrong, and musicians who are into Rush tend to be geeks who prattle on about unusual time signatures and innovative tunings, neither of which are within Francis's meager musical ability.

My band boyfriends always looked down on bands formed by students from the local music college as being technically precise and soulless, neither of which describes Francis, so the ten that mention it are also discarded.

We argue about bands who reference the White Stripes—I think this is great, since Francis informs me that the White Stripes don't have a bassist, so presumably they are thinking about burying Francis in the mix and just using him for his practice space and his transportation, but Francis says he wants to really play, so he tosses these.

Eventually we narrow it down to two that appear most promising: one band that mentioned the Ramones prominently, which earned them points, but then went on to cite Sum 41 and Blink-182, which made them suspect. Still, the Ramones reference gets them in. I think the most promising one is a guitarist who mentions early Who and Kinks as influences. This shows that he knows the best period for both bands, and that he is either steadfast in his refusal to cite any more recent bands that someone might consider cool, or else he's forty. Either one seems okay to me.

Francis has plenty of Ramones audition pieces, so we brainstorm for Who and Kinks songs that are obscure enough to make Francis seem like he knows more than "Lola" and "Pinball Wizard." Eventually we come up with "I'm a Boy" by the Who, and "David Watts" by the Kinks. Francis thinks "David Watts" is too obvious because the Jam covered it, and, for reasons I think are personal in nature, he wants to do "Stop Your Sobbing," which I don't think he'd be able to make it through without crying, or "Where Have All the Good Times Gone," but I convince him that picking a Kinks song that the Jam covered is way safer than one the Pretenders or Van Halen covered.

Francis heads home happy, and probably stays up all night practicing the songs in his basement, or, as he is fond of calling it, "My bassment! Get it! Bass like b-a-s-s!" He's hit both me and Chris with this awful pun, and hopefully he will use it on Angie the next time he talks to her and she will write him off as the old geek he is.

Not that I think he's an old geek—I just think anybody who's twenty-two should think he's an old geek. And I think he should stop trying to act like some kid that he really never was.

After he goes home, Chris and I are in bed, and Chris says, "It's good to see him interested in something. I can't remember him ever chasing anything in his life except for Lourdes. Everything else just kind of fell into his lap."

"I guess. I just wish he'd chase something more appropriate."

"Ahh, what the hell. Let the guy have some fun. He'll snap out of it eventually. He'll wake up with incredible lumbar pain after his first gig and realize he's thirty-five, and then he'll go to law school or something."

"But why can't he do that now? Why can't he be a grown-up? And why does he have to chase after this kid? It's . . . I don't know. It's unseemly."

Chris giggles. "Un*seem*ly? Did you just say something was un*seem*ly?"

"Yeah, well it is! And I don't know why that's funny!"

"I think that has to be the first time any member of your family has ever used that word seriously, unless it was your mom complaining that somebody said it about her attire."

Okay, he's laughed at me and invoked my mother at the same time. "You're just hoping he gets her so you can live vicariously through his big score."

"Oh, come on, hon, that's not fair. And anyway," he giggles, "he'll probably find the Webcam I planted over his bed long before that happens."

I punch him in his arm. Hard. "I love you, but you're pissing me off. Good night."

"Night, my only sweetest love." And he kisses me on my forehead. Asshole. But I'm not really mad at him. I'm mad at Francis. I'm afraid that he's going to be destroyed by his failure to be a rock god with Angie on his arm and I'm going to have to mop him up.

But I'm also jealous. I'm pushing forty, I'm fatter than I want to be, but I do work that matters, and I have a family that I love. And I guess I wouldn't trade my life for anything. Except that when we are sitting here falling asleep on our couch during *Fox 25 News at 10:00* every night, and I'm tending to kids and tending to dying people, I'd like to just be twenty-two again sometimes. I want to be pretty, I want to stay up too late and drink too much and, God help me, sleep with drummers again. (Okay, so that's why I picked Angie for a drummer fetishist. We know our own.) I don't want to live my life without Chris or Tommy or Dorothy, and I still love the explosion of love I feel for each of them at least once a day. And I was at peace with the fact that my youth was gone and never coming back. But now Francis has gone and gotten his back. And it's not fair.

I am the smallest, pettiest person on earth, and in view of what I have and Francis has lost, he should be jealous of me. But of course he's not, because, dopey crush, silly bass playing, horrible bassment pun and all, he's St. Francis, and I'm just Clare.

I turn this over for two hours, and finally I fall asleep.

TUESDAY IS FRANCIS'S audition with the guys who like the Who and the Kinks. The phone rings at 10:20, and I turn off *Fox 25 News at 10:00* over Chris's sleepy protest that hey, he was watching that, and answer the phone.

"Hello?" There's silence on the line, and a quiet little hiccup of a sob that I recognize as belonging to Francis. "Francis? What's wrong?"

"I . . . I had my audition tonight . . ." he says, and trails off into quiet sobbing.

Shit. This is exactly what I knew was going to happen. They probably clued into the fact that he's so old and rejected him before he even got to play. Or else he tried to play and sucked so bad that even his bassment and van couldn't convince them. And now, as predicted, I'm on clean-up duty. What I wouldn't have predicted is that I'm mad at these dumb-ass kids for being so mean to my brother who is so fragile, and not at all mad at him for his sad, mad dream of being a thirty-five-year-old punk rocker.

"Aw, sweetie, were they mean to you?" I ask.

"N . . . no . . . they were . . ." He's not in control of his voice, so it keeps getting suddenly higher as a sob tries to break through. I guess it might sound funny if it didn't sound like he was having his heart ripped out. ". . . very nice, actually . . ."

"But they rejected you?"

"N . . . no, I got the gig. I'm the new bassist for Happy Jack."

"Happy Jack?" Bands with names from other bands' songs are usually either horrible, or tribute bands, or both. "I mean, okay, but why are you, I mean . . ."

"Because I was really happy, and really excited, and all I wanted to do was tell my sweetie, and I can't tell my sweetie because she's dead, and that is so stupid, it's just the worst, stupidest . . ."—crying—". . . thing ever! I hate it! I mean, you know"—he manages to compose himself somewhat here—"this is really the first thing I've been happy about since she died, and then I found myself automatically thinking I would run upstairs and tell her, she'd be so happy for me . . ." And he trails off into more crying. There's nothing I can say.

Finally, he collects himself again. "It's not fair, Clare, it's not fair,

I liked my old life so much. I should be changing diapers now, not playing stupid bass in some stupid band! I should be going to mass, I should be getting my kid baptized, I should have some faith, I should be who I was! I don't even know this guy, this pathetic guy who only wants to play the bass with kids! I hate this!"

"I know, sweetie, I do. It's hateful. It's really really hateful, and I wish to God I could do something to make it less hateful."

"Yeah," he says. "Me too. I hate it. Did I mention that?"

"Yeah, you did. So are you going to take the job?"

"Well, it's not like I really have anything else going on in my life right now. I mean, what are my options? I hate God and the Cardinal, so that pretty well rules out the church. I have no wife, so I can't be a dad, which is what I really really want to do more than anything. So what else can I do?"

"I don't know, though you know lots of guys manage to be dads without having wives. I'm just saying." This raises a chuckle, which feels like a victory. "You could do something else where you get to work with kids. You could, I don't know, you could be a social worker, or a teacher or something."

"Well," he laughs, "it looks like I'm working with kids now. I don't know. I've been working really hard on this for quite a while. I mean, I don't do anything but play the bass and have the occasional meal with you. I literally played until my fingers bled. And now I've got what I wanted, and I don't really want it. But I guess I'll do it anyway."

"Okay. Well, maybe it'll be fun."

"I don't know. But it will get me out of the house late on Tuesday nights. I just want her back. It doesn't feel like that's too much to ask."

"I know. I'm sorry."

"Me too. I'm sorry I woke you up."

"Oh, well, I had to get off the couch and into the bed at some point."

"Okay. I guess I'm going to go to bed."

"Okay. Sleep well."

"Thanks. You too."

I E-MAIL MOM AND Dad with the Francis update, and I get separate, and very different, responses. Mom says she has trekked two miles to the nearest phone with long-distance capacity three times to call him but he never answers his phone, and so I have to convince him that he's wasting his gift here, that this is a ridiculous thing for him to be doing. Dad asks if I've heard the band, whether Francis can really play the bass, and if I still have his old original pressing of *Tommy* lying around somewhere.

I DECIDE I'VE PESTERED Francis enough on my own, so Mom is going to have to do her own heavy lifting. Anyway, I rarely see Francis for the next month. I don't have any patients within striking distance of his house, and he is always practicing, either alone or with the rest of the members of Happy Jack. He won't tell me much about how the practicing is going, whether he can actually play bass, or anything else, except that he gets to sing one cover song per set. He appears to be happy, and though I remember him crying when he got the job, I manage to stop myself from pestering him about whether he is truly deeply satisfied by this. He doesn't mention any dissatisfaction, and he does seem to enjoy learning to play songs he loves.

Also, he appears to like his bandmates a great deal. Their names are Ian and Ethan. Francis won't tell me much about them except that they are both twenty-four and have been in several other bands both together and apart. "They're really nice guys, really funny and really smart." He can't give me any examples of their being very funny or smart except that Ethan feels like his name is more trust fund than punk rock and is considering changing it to Lou Brickate. This starts me wondering if it was Francis's bassment joke that sealed the deal.

I do not practice an instrument during this time. I take Tommy to the ice rink a lot and try to teach him to skate, which is a challenge for me since I grew up in Cincinnati where nobody but the Cincinnati Stingers ice-skated. This, however, actually makes me a better skating coach than Chris, who grew up on skates in southern New Hampshire, and who is as hopeless at explaining how to skate as he would be at explaining how to walk.

Tommy and I fall a lot. After a few weeks, he's starting to get it. He skates away from me laughing one afternoon, and I want to save this moment forever in case I end up like Mrs. Cobb in Stoughton, nursing her twenty-five-year-old son, Eddie, to his death from Hodgkin's lymphoma.

I watch as Eddie goes from terrified to serene and his mom begins to fall apart. "I don't know where I'm going," Eddie says, "but I figure it's got to be good."

His mom corners me on my way out one day after taking Eddie's increasingly less vital signs. "You . . . I mean, you, you've seen this before, right? I mean parents losing their children?"

"All the time," I say.

"Is it . . . I mean how . . . I mean . . . every day I feel like my heart is breaking, and he's still here. How am I going to live when he's gone? What sense will anything make?"

"I don't know how you will do it, but I know you will. Everybody does."

She begins to cry, and she says, "My baby boy! My baby boy!" and I hug her and I think about my own baby boy. Please God, I think, don't do this to me, don't ever ever do this to me.

I always say a little prayer after I leave a patient's house, but this is the first time in a long time that I can't get through my prayer without crying. Soon I'm crying after I leave every house, which my boss, Helen, says is a sure sign that I need a vacation. I used a lot of time around Lourdes's death, but Helen is nice enough to give me more than I actually have coming. Chris and I start planning for a little getaway, and the Web searches and inevitable arguments help to fill up some mental space that might otherwise be devoted to freaking out. I am not above crying to get my way, which is how we end up with my dream vacation on a mountainside with nothing to do, instead of any of the three action-packed city getaways that Chris argues for.

FRANCIS CALLS ME one Wednesday and says, "Hey, can you come over for a couple of hours on Saturday? I have an errand I need you to help me with."

"Okay. What is it?" I ask.

"Uh, I'll tell you when you get here."

I'm intrigued and, of course, filled with trepidation, so Saturday morning I head over to Francis's house, and he greets me at the door and says, "Come on, let's take my van." We hug hello, and something feels different. I realize it's his arm.

"Have you been working out?" I ask, and Francis blushes.

"Yeah, I joined a gym. Ian and Ethan—"

"Don't you mean Lou Brickate?"

"He's off that—he's using the whole name, Ethan Walker Carrington III, now."

"Okay . . ." I guess he's operating on the "so un–punk rock it's punk rock" theory.

"Anyway, they like to play with their shirts off, and I just started to get self-conscious playing next to these totally buff guys, so I joined a gym."

"So you joined a gym so that you can play bass with your shirt off?"

"Basically, yeah." He's blushing again. "I know how dumb that is, so you really don't even have to tell me."

"I don't think it's dumb. Nothing that gets you out of that damn house is dumb. And exercise is healthy. But I still might have to tease you about it."

"Fair enough."

We get into Francis's van, which is actually a shiny new Honda Element with some kind of gigantic hard plastic case attached to the roof rack. It apparently hasn't been used to haul any gear to gigs yet, since Happy Jack is just (Francis informs me) burning some CDs from some live four-track recordings they made in his bassment in hopes of getting some gigs. He goes on at length about his new computer, and some kind of software called Pro Tools, and something about mixing the CD, and he bores me to death, so I just look at the people in the other cars for a few minutes.

He also won't tell me where we are going. After driving around for twenty minutes, we manage to find a parking space in Boston's South End, which is a nice little miracle.

We park the car and walk a few blocks on brick sidewalks until we reach a storefront where Francis turns and starts going in.

"Oh, no, Francis, no, really, no, please tell me this is not happening."

"It's happening!" he says, and turns into INK, which, apparently, is a tattoo parlor. On the inside, it's clean and well lit, all black Formica, glass, and chrome. There are examples of tattoo art all over the walls and inside the L-shaped glass counters. My eye is caught by a shark with a crown of thorns looking heavenward while a disembodied pair of praying hands dripping blood hovers in front of him. "Just tell me you're not getting the shark," I say to Francis, but he's already talking to the young woman at the register, who is wearing a black T-shirt with *INK* in bold white letters and who sports multicolored tattoos all over her arms, saying, "I have an appointment with Raven?"

"Great. I'll get her."

Raven emerges, and my first thought is that she is me if I had dropped out of school, continued to sleep with drummers, and taken up tattooing as a career. So she's about forty, her hair is long and dyed Elvis-black, and she is, it should go without saying, covered with ink, all black and in various Celtic and Christian symbols. She is, of course, dressed in all-black (I wonder if that's a house rule here at INK, and whether you are allowed to wear, for example, pink if you have taken to calling yourself Raven), and, like me at Angie's gig, she's just a little too old and fat to be a credible rock chick. Except, unlike me, she appears to be completely comfortable in her ink-stained skin, so she actually can carry the look off.

"Hey, Francis. You ready?"

"Yeah, I'm ready. This is my sister, Clare. She's here for moral support."

"Okay. Come on back."

We walk through a beaded curtain into what appears to be a filthy dentist's office. The back has been broken into little cubicles with thin white walls that do not appear to be cleaned very regularly. Each cubicle has a dentist's chair, and Raven's has a mezuzah on the doorway, two strings of multicolored Tibetan prayer flags hanging from the drop ceiling, a crucifix on the wall, and pictures of Raven at Stonehenge, Notre Dame, the Wailing Wall, and what is either an Asian monastery or the set of a kung fu movie. "Places of power," she says as she takes her seat and starts pulling her supplies from her cabinet.

Francis sits down in the chair and hands me two rolls of Pep-O-Mint Life Savers. "Here. Administer these when necessary."

"Uh, okay." Part of me wants to make a scene here, to tell Francis that he's making an irrevocable decision, that I hope he knows what he's doing, that men his age don't get tattoos, that he's going to be limiting the kinds of jobs he can get when the whole Happy Jack thing doesn't pan out, that he is crazy and stupid . . .

And yet he is, in all respects, acting less like a crazy person than he has in quite a while. And I've grown uncomfortable in the role of the disapproving grown-up, so I think I may just have to grit my teeth and go along with whatever insanity grips Francis at any given moment. Maybe this will help with my rock chick attitude. Also, I hate to admit it, but I can hear Chris's voice telling me that this is good for Francis in some way, and so I guess I'll sit here and give him mints. Whatever those are for.

Raven wipes Francis's right forearm with an alcohol swab and then shaves it with a disposable Bic. Forearm, Francis? I want to yell. Forearm? You couldn't pick anything more discreet?

I say nothing.

She slaps a little stencil on his arm, and there's suddenly a carbon-paper image of Our Lady of Lourdes on his forearm, complete with the "Je Suis L'Immaculate Conception" around her head. I find it somewhat reassuring—it's a connection to his old life. Maybe it's a tombstone for his old life, but at least it's a connection to Lourdes. It seems like he's found a way to link his wannabe rocker life to what I think of as his real life, though of course what he has now is his real life.

Over the next two and a half hours, Raven administers the tattoo (using fresh ink and a sterile, one-use needle, I note approvingly). Francis grits his teeth and crunches the Pep-O-Mint Life Savers, and I am suddenly, powerfully reminded of standing in our parents' closet crunching Pep-O-Mint Life Savers and watching the sparks in each other's mouths nearly thirty years ago.

Except then there were not tears leaking out of Francis's eyes as there are now. He doesn't make a sound—he just scrunches up his face and squeezes the tears out of the corner of his eyes and crunches the Life Savers, and Raven inks and wipes the blood away, and eventually Our Lady of Lourdes is complete in full color on Francis's right forearm. The skin around the tattoo is pink, and Raven applies a bandage and gives Francis a sheet with care instructions and some ointment to put on it.

"Well, I hate to say this, but it looks great," I say, and it really does. I can picture him playing the bass with this on his right forearm, and I think even if the Angie thing falls through, he will probably have girls swarming around him constantly. More than likely they won't be the kind of girls I'd like for him to be dating, but maybe Chris is right again, and he deserves some fun. "How does it feel?"

"It hurts a lot. It feels good."

"So, uh, why'd you decide to get it?"

"I . . . uh . . . I don't know. I can't explain it. I mean, part of it was to fit in, okay, which I am not proud of, but also it just felt like . . . I dunno. I'm having fun now, you know, but I still feel like my life is over, like this life is just some kind of joke. And it's a good joke, it's definitely one I enjoy, but it doesn't feel real. What feels real is Lourdes. So I guess I wanted to have something that felt real for her—to remind me of what's real. Or what was real, or something."

"Well," I say. "It looks good."

"Thanks."

We get back in the car and head back to Francis's house, where he assures me he's going to cook me lunch. I'm convinced that this means he's going to heat something in the microwave, but he actually digs into his fridge and pulls out some chicken and vegetables and creates a credible stir-fry, though he winces every time he tries to stir with his freshly tattooed arm.

"So how are you?" he asks, which has to be the first time in months he's asked me that question.

"I don't know. I'm . . . I need a vacation, I think. I've been crying a lot, after I leave every patient, which can't really be healthy. So I guess Chris and I are going to ditch the kids with his folks and go to Vermont for a week."

"Well, that sounds great—I still have a bunch of bike maps, if you want to borrow some."

"No thanks. Neither one of us is very outdoorsy, which probably makes this a bad choice. I just rented us a house on a mountain where we can sit and do nothing for a week."

"When are you leaving?"

"Next Thursday."

"Great! So you can come to our gig!" Oh God. Let me guess. Another Tuesday night at midnight.

"When and where?"

"Tuesday night at Mister Punchy's."

"Where the hell is that? I've never heard of that place."

"I guess it's new. It's in the South End." Great. No place to park, and parts of the South End, including, I'm sure, the nongentrified parts where they can put a punk rock club, can be pretty dicey at night, especially down by the hospital where the whores and junkies and, probably, punk rockers congregate.

"Midnight?"

"No, we're actually supposed to go on at ten."

"Wow! How'd you swing that?"

"I guess our demo sounds pretty good or something."

"So." Why do I even bring this up? What is wrong with me? "Is Angie going to be there?"

"No, I don't think so. Mary's Cherry is playing the Middle East that night."

"Do you talk to her often?"

"Yeah, we have coffee once a week. And yes, I have an enormous crush on her, and no, I haven't done anything except have coffee and I haven't made a fool of myself, though I do think she might be interested. I mean, we have pretty good conversations."

But Francis, I want to say, you just don't play the drums. Then again, neither did Chris.

"And I think she's getting discouraged with the whole band thing. She asked me to read an application essay for grad school."

"What's she want to study?"

"She's thinking of being a teacher, but I don't think she knows if that's something she really wants to do or if she's just falling into it because her parents are teachers."

"Hmm." She's clearly confiding in him, which could be the beginning of something, or could be setting up the old "I think of you as a brother" play. Which I actually considered running on Chris at one point. So, basically, I can't get anything valuable from Francis's description. I can't even tell if the glacial speed at which he's moving is a plus—"He's wearing her down!"—or a minus—"His window of opportunity is closing!"

I finish my lunch and head home. Chris and I decide that since we are imposing on his parents for an entire week, we can't really hit them up for another Tuesday night rock and roll baby-sitting experience, so he's going to stay home and I'm going to venture out to Mister Punchy's by myself.

Tuesday night comes, and, inspired by Raven, I decide to wear my "too old and fat to be cool" rock club outfit with pride. I'm not quite sure I'm pulling it off, which probably means I'm not. I find Mister Punchy's on Washington Street, which is considerably nicer now than I remember it being from my city-dwelling days. Mister Punchy's sits between some kind of yuppie bakery and a video store with pictures for the latest indie releases in the front window. It's certainly not the scummy, junkie-infested hole I thought it might be.

The bouncer does not ID me, but he does look at me kind of funny, and I brace myself for him to ask me whose mother I am. Thankfully, he says nothing, and I pay my eight-dollar cover and go in. Mister Punchy's is long and skinny, and a fairly unremarkable bar—it does not appear to have the layers of filth I expect in a rock and roll club, nor does it really have a stage: there is a little riser in the back of the bar where Francis, Ian, and Ethan are setting up. I wave at Francis, and he gives me a short, nervous wave and goes back to plugging stuff in. I go to the bar and order a beer, and then I find a seat at a table. And I realize something feels a little off about this place. It's dark and, as I said, nondescript, and there is a television behind the bar, and the walls are paneled with some kind of light wood, and there are even little baskets of popcorn on the small round wooden tables. So what's wrong?

I sip my beer and look around, and then it hits me. It's not the thin Tuesday night crowd—that's fairly normal—it's that there are no other women in this entire bar. Now, admittedly, I make up about fifteen percent of the clientele right now, but still—where are the women?

Then it hits me—I realize I'm in the South End, there are no women here—I'm in a gay bar. My brain still won't make the obvious connection, and so I think something like, "Wow, they must have cast a really wide net looking for gigs, they even sent the CD to this tiny gay bar—no wonder they didn't get the midnight slot."

And then Ethan, done setting up, steps to the mike and says, "Hi everybody, thanks for coming out, we're Happy Jack, and this one's called 'Astroglide,' " and I realize that my brother has joined a gay punk band. I really don't know whether to laugh or cry, because this is just so completely absurd. He's joined a band with the chief goal of impressing girls, and he's going to be the first straight man in the history of rock and roll to join a band and get absolutely no pussy as a result.

As if on cue, another dozen or so handsome young men pour through the front door and head straight for the stage. Instantly this goes from a standard pathetic Tuesday night gig to a spectacularly successful Tuesday night gig, and the effect on Happy Jack's enthusiasm is obvious. The drummer starts playing faster, Francis actually manages to keep up with him, and "Astroglide" finishes up big.

They power through a dozen more songs, and while they are a little rough in spots—they have three different false starts, and they are just a little sloppy throughout—the songs are catchy, poppy, funny songs that sound for the most part like they were co-written by Ray Davies and Dee Dee Ramone.

Now, admittedly, the band is not playing anything very demanding from a musical standpoint, but Francis acquits himself very well. He plays credibly and only causes one of the three false starts and is not the obvious drag on the band that you might expect the thirty-five-year-old who owns the van to be.

And, unbelievably, he looks cool. Now, I am probably the only one who notices this, because both Ethan and Ian are muscular tattooed young Adonises, and Ethan sings all the songs and has fantastic stage presence. I have to keep reminding myself to pay attention to Francis, because my eyes keep going back to Ethan.

But Francis is there in his Dee Dee Ramone stance, legs wide apart, bass slung low in front of his crotch, and he doesn't have much room to move around, but he bobs his head, lunges with the bass, and doesn't look phony or awkward doing it. He's wearing black Converse high-tops just like the ones Dee Dee was wearing the night Francis touched his feet, and he's wearing tight jeans that are ripped at the knee, and a black T-shirt with the words "What Would Dee Dee Do?" emblazoned across his chest.

Dee Dee, of course, would turn tricks for dope, have destructive, unhealthy relationships with women, and die with a syringe next to him, all of which would be repugnant to Francis, but I have to admit that it is pretty punk rock. Our Lady of Lourdes hops up and down as Francis plays, and that also looks cool.

Happy Jack finishes up what might well be a hit single called "I Wanna Get Married." (Ethan growls out, "My wife looks just like Dick Van Patten/He's picking out our china pattern," and I laugh out loud. I then wonder how a kid Ethan's age even knows who Dick Van Patten is, and I hope Francis wrote that line.) Francis nervously steps to the mike and says, "This is the old-school song from the old man. One, two, three, four!" and the band launches into the Buzzcocks' "What Do I Get?"

The band is particularly sloppy on this number—they obviously haven't given it the same attention as the originals—but Francis does it really well. His singing voice is thin but credible, and certainly light-years better than Dee Dee Ramone's ever was.

"I just want a lover like any other, what do I get," he sings, "I only want a friend to stay till the end, what do I get," and though the band is not very tight, he is really putting his heart into it. I actually find myself tearing up, because except for possibly Ethan and Ian, I am the only person in the bar who fully understands why Francis picked this cry against the unfairness of not having the one you love for his first public cover song. I am in the middle of a gay bar with my ears ringing and the smell of beer, sweat, and cologne in my nostrils, and all I can think of is Lourdes dying and Francis howling. He's still howling.

Francis's star turn finishes up with the great call-and-response part of the end of this song, where Ethan and Ian go, "What do I get?" and Francis answers, "Nothing that's nice . . . no love at all . . . 'cause I don't get you!," and I find myself screaming that rock fan "Woooooo!" and standing up before I even know what I'm doing. I'm just so freaking proud of him.

Ethan retakes the mike, but not before the entire band strip their shirts off. They manage to look like they're doing it just because it's really hot in here, but Francis shoots me a look that reveals that he knows there's an eye-candy marketing moment going on here. And Francis definitely looks thin and somewhat underdeveloped next to Ethan and especially Ian, who has those big muscular drummer arms, and I am glad that my rational brain is insisting that Ian must be gay, because my reptile brain wants to climb up onstage and jump him.

Three more songs, and they finish with a number Ian introduces as "Kicked Out of Boarding School," which doesn't seem like a very punk rock song subject, but which they manage to pull off chiefly by making a lot of very obvious "oral examination" jokes. (The best rhyme of the song is "existentialist fiction" with "top marks for my DICK . . . tion.")

The crowd applauds enthusiastically, I find myself wooooo-ing again, and I am really glad that I don't have to lie to Francis about what I thought of the gig when he comes to sit with me.

The equipment is unpacked, and Ethan, Ian, and, to a lesser degree, Francis have to fight their way through a group of starstruck young men to get off the stage. Francis eventually joins me at the table with a gigantic plastic tumbler full of seltzer. He looks like he always used to look when he just got off his bike—flushed, sweaty, and elated.

"So?" he said. "What did you think? Did you like it? How was I?"

"I really enjoyed it. I mean, I really did. You guys are still a little rough around the edges, but you're pretty good together, and the songs are great."

"Yeah, Ethan and Ian write them all. I think they're great."

"Did you give him the Dick Van Patten line?"

"Yeah, we were brainstorming rhymes with 'china pattern.' "

"All those hours watching *Eight Is Enough* weren't wasted after all."

"Yeah. How'd you like my song?"

"It made me cry."

"Seriously."

"No, seriously! I felt like you were singing about her, and it was just genuinely very touching."

"Thanks!" He's beaming.

"So, uh, why didn't you tell me this is a gay band?"

"I just didn't want to tell you anything about the band before you saw us. I wanted you to come in with a clean slate so you could really look at us objectively."

"So are Ian and Ethan . . ."

"A couple? I think they're kind of on-again off-again. It doesn't seem like the most incredibly stable relationship, but I think that causes some creative tension that's good for the band."

"Um . . . okay."

"And we're playing all gay clubs this month—it's really brilliant marketing—the idea is that we build up this loyal fan base who will then come out to the other clubs and not make us look like a loser band with three fans."

I resist pointing out that he's just labeled his would-be girlfriend's band a loser band.

"Well, I guess it's a good strategy. But, um, aren't you going to have a hard time impressing the ladies in a band like this?"

"Hey!" He waves a piece of paper at me. "I got digits from a pre-op transsexual! I'm pretty sure that in a few months that will count as impressing a lady."

"Okay, but Angie . . ."

"Angie knows I'm not gay."

"Really? Because if she thinks you're gay, she might feel free to get all huggy and stuff, and treat you like a confidant, and you might misinterpret, and—"

"She knows I was married!"

"That's not the same as knowing you're straight."

"Uh. Well, she'll figure it out." I hope he's right, and I have to stop and realize that I just hoped he was right, that this stupid rock and roll dream works out, complete with the twenty-two-year-old babe. I must be intoxicated by the music.

THE NEXT DAY, Chris and I head to Vermont. We bring only Chris's cell phone, which he has pledged to answer only if his mom calls about the kids. The cabin on the side of a mountain turns out to be a modern-looking ski condo and not at all the log cabin I wanted. Our isolation, however, turns out to be pretty complete. We bring groceries, and Chris pledges not to watch the satellite TV when I'm anywhere near it.

He gets quite a few hours of TV in early, though. As soon as we arrive, I start crying hysterically. Chris tries in vain to get me to explain what the hell is wrong, but it's nothing specific—I just seem to have been sitting on a lot of sadness for a long time, and maybe because I don't have to see anybody who's dying for a week, or maybe because Francis is finally starting to get kind of healthy in his own strange second adolescence way, it all comes pouring out.

I fall asleep and sleep for twelve hours. Chris apparently gets a good amount of satellite TV in during this time, because he doesn't complain for the rest of the week, even on Saturday afternoon when the BC football game is on, and, God bless him, he doesn't even ask me if he can watch it.

On Sunday we drive forty minutes to the nearest Catholic church. This being Vermont, there are guitars and a flute involved in the service. Before we take our seats, I light a candle for Lourdes and one for Francis. The mass is uneventful, but as I walk back from getting the host, crunching the body of Christ, I feel serene for the first time in months, possibly for the first time since the healing mass in Lourdes's room. I do think God is here with me, and with Francis, and with all of my patients who may or may not die while I'm on vacation. Why is this feeling so hard to hang on to?

The rest of the week goes by quickly in a haze of spy novels and spontaneous, energetic sex. It is really amazing what you can accomplish and where you can accomplish it when you are not sharing a house with two children.

When we get back, reality tumbles back onto me. One of my patients died while I was away, and I feel bad about not being there for her, especially when I see all my other patients' faces light up when they see that I'm back. I say a brief prayer after I leave every house, but I do not cry.

There are messages from Francis. Happy Jack has had two more gigs in the last week, also at gay bars, and Francis has apparently been deluged with phone numbers of eligible men. He's also sorry that he missed so many Sunday dinners, and could he please come this week, he promises not to miss any more but he really misses us and he owes Tommy a gigantic noogie.

So Francis comes over, and once the kids have run away from the dinner table, Chris says, "So, what's the deal with your jailbait girl-friend?"

Now if I came out with a line like that, Francis would need to argue that she is neither jailbait nor his girlfriend, but somehow he and Chris have this kind of thing worked out, and he just smiles and says, "I think she's going to ask me to her prom."

"Eww, Francis, that's kind of gross."

"Yes. No, she's fine, I think her band is breaking up. I saw them last week, and she and the drummer were kind of looking daggers at each other the whole time, while the bassist rolled his eyes. When their set was over he threw his bass down, walked offstage, and yelled his resignation at them."

Please, please, please tell me Francis is not going to be the new bassist for Mary's Cherry. Especially if he's walking into the middle of her breakup with her drummer. Please, please, please . . .

"She asked me if I wanted to play with them, but I said no."

"Wow! Why?"

"Well, I do still have pathetic designs on her, and watching what happens whenever Ian and Ethan are mad at each other, I think having a couple in a band might not be a good idea."

"I thought that produced creative tension that was good for the band."

"Yeah. As it turns out, it produces tension that is a pain in the butt for the third wheel."

"So do you think you'll stay with that band?" Chris says.

"Oh, definitely. It fills up my days and nights and gives me something to think about besides why God hates me and how incredibly much I miss Lourdes. Well, I actually think about both things all the time, but I imagine it would be even worse if I didn't have this to do."

For some reason, this comment unlocks my inner busybody. I go to the kitchen to make coffee to stop myself from telling Francis that he has to go talk to a priest, or a rabbi, or a minister, or an imam, or somebody who can help him sort this God thing out. I realize that I used up most of my "you have to do this" points when I screamed at him to go to therapy, so I just grind coffee beans and my teeth.

And then, on Tuesday, I decide to go see Father Tim. I don't even tell Chris about this, because I know exactly what he would say to me: "Jesus, hon, will you just leave well enough alone? He's doing something he likes, he's happy, and he might bag a hottie! Of course he's still messed up, but it hasn't even been a year yet! He's a grown-up! Leave him alone!" One of the benefits of being married is that I can get Chris's advice without the difficulty of actually asking him for it and the additional difficulty of arguing with him about it while knowing that he's right.

So if I know he's right, what am I doing here in the rectory? I don't know. I just . . . yes I do. I owe my faith to him, and my faith is what gets me through my life. Francis did this for me, and it was the biggest gift he ever gave me, and I feel like I owe it to him.

Father Tim is forty-five, thin, and has reddish brown hair. I find him in his small, dark office, which is lit by one dim desk lamp. He gives me a hug, and before I can unleash my canned speech about Francis, he cuts me off.

"I guess you're here to ask me if I can talk to Francis and get him to go back to mass, to forgive God, all that stuff?"

"Um, yeah."

"Well, I beat you to it. After Lourdes died, I gave him a few months, and then I started calling him every week, asking if he wanted to meet me for coffee, talk about stuff, if he wanted to come and sit in with the youth group—which has lost half its members since Francis left, by the way—something to get him hooked in."

"And what happened? He didn't tell me any of this."

"Well, he finally agreed to meet me for coffee. He paid, which was nice. I got a double skim latte, he got black coffee, and he said he couldn't go back to church because of the Cardinal and because God had kicked him in the teeth."

"Yeah. That's pretty much what he said to me too. I never really have any good arguments for him, though. I mean, the Cardinal is horrible, and it's easy for me to say he should forgive God, because I still have my spouse."

"And I, of course, never had one. I did tell him that I continue to be a priest because I am serving God, not because I serve the Cardinal. But he wasn't buying."

"So what can we do?"

"I don't think there's anything we can do. I gave him some Bible verses to look at, I gave him some books about grief, but I don't think he's reading any of it. He really feels like God is a friend who has betrayed him. But I do think God will continue to call to him, and I think he will hear the call one day."

I thank Father Tim, promise to stay in touch, and walk out into the street. I wonder if God is calling Francis. I wonder what that sounds like. I wonder if he will listen.

For now, though, God appears to be on hold, and Francis is focusing on playing with Happy Jack. They play several more gigs, which I don't attend by reason of being an adult. The marketing scheme is working, though, according to Francis. Once they played at their first nongay club on a Tuesday night, they brought fifty fans in, and the club immediately booked them for three more shows.

Tommy gets sick, I get busy, Chris takes a business trip, and Dorothy is afflicted with the Coxsackie virus, a hellish, but not life-threatening, thing that gives her horribly painful sores in her mouth. I spend the better part of a week fighting her in an attempt to get liquid into her mouth so she doesn't dehydrate. When I "win," I get her to suck on a popsicle for about fifteen seconds before she starts screaming.

About a week after the Coxsackie episode ends, Chris turns to me after dinner and says, "Well, I hope it goes well."

"You hope what goes well?"

"You know!" I have no idea what he's talking about and look at him blankly, wondering if I have forgotten something really important that was supposed to happen tonight, or a performance review at work, or something. "Francis . . ." he offers.

"What, does he have a gig tonight or something?"

"No, it's a Wednesday. They are so over playing Wednesdays. Don't you ever listen when he has dinner here?"

"I guess I kind of space out when he starts talking about all the band logistics."

"No, this is the Angie thing."

"What Angie thing?"

"Oh . . . Oh, boy, I didn't . . . he didn't tell you, did he?"

"Tell me what? What the hell are you talking about?"

"Well, he called me today to ask for some advice, because he's decided that it's finally time for him to make his move on Angie, now that she and the drummer are broken up." Whoa. Not only did Francis call Chris for romantic advice, he admitted I was right about the drummer and never told me! I'm going to kill him!

I'm having a hard time putting words together here, so I just kind of sputter for a few seconds until Chris steps in with "So I told him he should just be direct, you know, not try to kiss her without talking about it first, just tell her how he feels, and hopefully she'll say she feels the same way, and away they go!"

"I . . . ugh . . . so when is he . . . how is he . . ." I am picturing all kinds of horrible, awkward scenarios that involve Francis lighting candles, cooking something from a cookbook, and being humiliated.

"She's playing a show tonight with the new Mary's Cherry. Francis says this version can actually play, and Angie is rethinking grad school. He's going to drop the bomb after the show."

I have no idea what to make of all this. Why didn't he call me? Am I driving a wedge between us with my skepticism? And do I hope he succeeds, or fails? I think about this, and I decide I have to go with succeeds. If he fails, he's going to be miserable. If he succeeds . . . well, I'll probably have to have Angie over for dinner, and I suppose there are worse things. And he'll be happy, sort of, for a while. Or else he'll get to kiss her and realize that she's not what he needs to fill up his life, and he'll be miserable. Or . . . I suppose there are two possible good outcomes, which are that they have a short, fun fling that ends by mutual agreement, or else they get married and live happily ever after. The only problem is that I don't really see either one happening.

If I weren't still paying off a sleep debt, I might stay up worrying about this. And if I weren't so busy, I might find time during the following day to call him before nine at night. I don't know what to make of the fact that he didn't call. Either they are wearing each other out in bed, or he's crushed. Once the kids are in bed, I say a little prayer that Angie will be in his bed when I call, that I won't have to mop him up.

"Francis," I say when he picks up the phone.

"Hey," he says in a flat, most definitely not-worn-out-from-humping voice.

Shit. I am going to have to go into town and kill either Angie for breaking my baby brother's heart, or Francis for being such a dope.

"So, do you want to talk about it?"

"She . . . she . . . oh, God, I am so humiliated. She had this look— I mean, I said that I really wanted us to be more than friends, and she had this look, this . . . she was shocked. It never even crossed her mind! Ugh. I'm such an idiot!"

His voice breaks a little, and I'm really afraid he's going to cry. Now I know this bitch is not good enough for him. How could she not have seen this coming? Maybe she's not used to guys who are interested in her doing anything other than grunting through their beer belches or something. I will kill her. Scratch her stupid, naive, "oh I really have no idea how sexy I am" face off.

"Aw, Francis, I'm sorry."

"She said she thought of me as a big brother! A big brother! Christ!" Oh, she ran the "love you like a brother" play.

"And she said all kinds of stuff about how she valued my opinion, and she respected me, and she wanted us to be friends"—and, let me guess, that some girl would be very lucky to have him—"and that I'd make somebody very happy. God, I'm such an idiot, Clare, I'm such a fucking idiot, I want to die, I just want to die!"

"No you don't."

"I do! I made a complete fool of myself, I wasted months, I got a tattoo! A tattoo! Which is going to be on my arm forever!" So as it turns out, Francis's explanation when he got the tattoo was a lie. He got it to impress a girl. Which should make its continued presence on his arm a real source of joy in years to come. I should have told him not to get it! I went along and didn't say anything!

"So, uh, how'd you get out of it?"

"I was mean, Clare, I feel bad. I should probably apologize. I'll send her a note or something."

"What did you say?" I am remembering Francis's acid tongue after Lourdes's funeral and kind of hoping he left a mark when he used it this time.

"I told her I already had a sister, and I got up and walked out." Good for him! That's what the bitch gets for running "I think of you as a brother" on my brother!

"I don't think you need to apologize. That's about the best she could have hoped for."

Now, finally, he's crying, full-on. "What am I going to do, Clare, I'm a loser, I'm a total loser, I am exactly the kind of loser you thought I would be, except it's worse! I have nothing! Nothing!"

"That's not true. You have a bunch of phone numbers. Did your pre-op ever get her operation?" This provokes what I think is a laugh breaking through the crying. "And you have me, and Chris, your romantic counselor who is now oh-for-one, and Tommy and Dorothy, and God help me, I think you are a real bass player now."

"Sid Vicious was a real bass player! That doesn't mean anything!"

"And when Sid Vicious was your age, he was dead. You're still here, and I'm glad you're here, and someday soon there will be a girl, there will probably be a lot of girls. I actually think you can play this gay band thing to your advantage, because you could probably convince a bunch of girls that they were converting you."

"That would be dishonest. But I guess that's what women want."

"Well, not all women. But definitely some."

More sniffing. "Will you . . . we're playing on Saturday night, we're opening for the Spines at Valhalla on Friday, will you come, please? And bring Chris? I was . . . I was going to guest-list Angie, but I don't really think she'll be coming."

I MANAGE TO GET an actual teen baby-sitter for Saturday night, which is far more miraculous than finding a parking space in the South End, so I manage to avoid hitting up Chris's mom again.

Chris and I drive to Allston to go to Valhalla, and this is a very stupid move, because Allston parking is the worst in the entire city of Boston, and we end up parking a half mile from the club in a resident parking zone, so we can be guaranteed to add the cost of a parking ticket to this evening.

But, what the hell, the concert is free.

When we get to Valhalla, assorted cool-looking people in their twenties are milling around outside, most of them smoking. A few of them, to judge by the smell, are actually smoking clove cigarettes, which shoots me right back to my Jockey Club days.

We head for the door, and we stand in a line of heavily pierced young people who are all giving us that "what the hell are you doing here" look. I am not wearing my rock club gear, but just my normal hanging out clothes—jeans and a T-shirt from Graeter's Ice Cream in Cincinnati. Chris is wearing his rock club gear, which is to say jeans and a red polo again.

When we get up to the door, the bouncer asks us for tickets, and I get to say, "We're on the guest list—Clare and Chris Hayes." I feel so cool right now that I wish I was wearing my rock club outfit, because I'm sure I could put Raven to shame in terms of carrying off the attitude. I feel like turning to the assembled pierced masses behind me and going, "That's right! The old people are on the guest list! And you paid for a ticket like a sucker! Hah!"

The club is a definite step up from Mister Punchy's. For one thing, it is huge—there is a real rock and roll stage, and a decent-sized floor in front of it, and three levels of seats and tables. It looks like the place could probably hold over five hundred people.

And right now it's probably holding half that, which I know from my years as a club rat is a big deal. Because nobody who's anybody shows up before the opening band goes on. That "doors at eight" business is for dorks and old people.

But it's eight-thirty, and there's already a substantial crowd milling around. Happy Jack's equipment is already set up, and I notice that Ian now has "Happy Jack" emblazoned on his bass drum, which means this band is stuck with this crappy name pretty much forever.

I spoke to Francis this morning, and he was in an emotional state that makes me a little afraid of what's to come tonight. He was just incredibly depressed and lethargic, and not at all excited about playing the biggest show he's ever played. It was a lot of "I have nothing, my life is a joke," punctuated by "I wouldn't even play the stupid show if the guys weren't counting on me."

So I hope Francis doesn't blow the big gig. I look around and notice that probably fifty people here are wearing Happy Jack T-shirts.

They are black, of course, and say HAPPY JACK in white on the front (clearly the product of the same design genius who makes the INK shirts). On the back, they sport different song titles in block letters: I WANNA GET MARRIED, KICKED OUT OF BOARD-ING SCHOOL, and what appears to be a new number called P-TOWN SUCKS, which I suppose could be either praise or criti-cism. Under the song title, there is a comic-book-style line drawing of the band. And there's Francis! My baby brother is on a T-shirt! I can't believe he hasn't given me one!

I continue scanning the crowd while Chris goes to brave the bar and get us beers. At a table back in the corner, I see somebody I am almost certain is Angie, but it's very dim in here, and I'm not about to go over there to find out, because I might find myself going, "Get the hell out of here! How's he going to get over you if you show up at stuff like this!" But why is she here? Surely she's not actually try-ing to maintain their friendship?

I intend to ask my husband, Dr. Love, his opinion, but when he returns, he's carrying two Happy Jack T-shirts. "They're selling them over by the bar!" he says.

"But we could have gotten them for free!"

"Yeah, but I thought we could show some support. The concert's free, anyway." He's right, except when you add up the cost of the baby-sitter, the inevitable parking ticket, and the T-shirts, it's com-ing to way more than the price of two tickets.

Our Happy Jack T-shirts say TO HELL WITH THE CARDINAL on the back. "I figure this has to be one that Francis wrote," Chris says, and I hope it's true. I have to ask him about it.

But first I'm going to the bathroom to put my new T-shirt on. Which is something I would have found way too dorky to do when I was a regular concertgoer, but now I am a dorky concertgoer, so nothing is beneath me. The bathroom is small with black Formica stalls with doors that actually lock and that have only one or two band stickers each, and the mirror sports no Magic Marker graffiti at all. Capacity issues aside, this really shows that Happy Jack has hit a completely different level of venue.

When I emerge from the stall with my Happy Jack T-shirt on and my Graeter's T-shirt in my hand, I run into Angie. Literally. I bump into her and am halfway through my "Oh my God I'm so sorry" before I notice who it is.

"Hey! You're Clare, right? Francis's sister?"

"Yeah," I say coolly, and if there were more room in here, I would sweep out at this point, leaving her to contemplate her crime. But I'd have to squeeze past some girl who appears to have an infected tongue stud and is examining the discharge in the mirror, and that is just not something I want to do right now.

And then I am glad for the girl's infected stud, because Angie starts to cry, and I feel kind of bad for wanting to walk out on her. I am also, of course, annoyed. Do I have some kind of sign on my back that says, "Cry to Me"? Or do my ears just look especially sympathetic? And then she starts to sniff and babble, and I think she is obviously perfect for Francis, who was sniffing and babbling at me only this morning.

I put a hand on her shoulder, and she looks at me gratefully. "I fucked up," she says. "I mean, I never meant for him to think, I mean, I thought he was a grown-up, you know, and I'm just this kid, it never even crossed my mind . . ."

She seems like she's about twelve years old right now. Why couldn't Francis see this? He never would have wanted to actually date somebody this young. Would he?

Tongue Stud Discharge Girl is looking over with a lot of interest. If I were even a little drunk, I'd tell her to pay more attention to her oral hygiene and less to us, but as it is I just shoot her a look, which does not stop her from staring at me.

I don't really know what to say—you walk around with a body like that and don't think men are going to be interested? What the hell's wrong with you? But then I remember everything I said to Francis about how he was this authority figure to her, and how this whole thing was kind of creepy, and it's starting to look like I was right. This gives me no satisfaction at all. I have to say something, so I say, "Well, uh, you know, Francis still isn't really himself. Or, anyway, he's some version of himself that none of us really recognize very well. So he's a little bit nuts, you know."

"I guess I can understand that. It's just that"—sniff, sniff—"I like hate my parents, and that feeling is pretty mutual, my big sister just got her MBA, and we don't talk unless snapping across the Thanksgiving table counts, and I just"—more sniffing, and a nose wipe, with a tissue I've provided, because moms always have tissues, even when they go out to rock clubs, because you just never know—"I don't have anybody. Anybody . . . My stupid boyfriend left me, I don't know what I'm going to do with my life . . ."

And Tongue Stud suddenly says, "You're better off without him. Everybody I know slept with him, including me," and then she leaves.

Angie and I stare at each other blankly. "Do you know that girl?"

"No, but they all seem to know me, the stupid one whose boyfriend they fucked."

"Well, if he was really sleeping with skanks like that, you are better off without him."

"I know! But I'm not better off without Francis! He always had these like good ideas about stuff, he listened to me whine about what I was going to do with my life . . . he was like, I don't know, my like mentor or something. And I don't even know what I did to make him think . . ." And she's off again.

I let her cry for a minute, and then I say, "Francis is not the kind of person to stay mad forever. He was already composing his apology letter on Thursday night." And I discouraged him from writing it, but I don't tell her that.

Eventually Angie calms down, and God help me, I give her my phone number and my e-mail, and I tell her that it's going to be fine, and we head back outside, and she goes over to her table where she's sitting with the reconstituted Mary's Cherry. The guy she points out as the drummer is looking at her like a puppy dog, which hopefully indicates he's an upgrade from the previous drummer.

Chris is standing there looking kind of lost as young hipsters mill around him. I sneak up behind him and hug him around the waist and try to just think about the show and not be too sad about Francis and Angie, these two pathetic lost souls, and how I may actually get saddled with both of them.

After another ten minutes, the lights go down and a disembodied voice says, "Ladies and Gentlemen, welcome to Valhalla Rock Club. Please welcome Boston's own Happy Jack!"

Now, I have been to any number of rock shows and heard this same announcement with different club and band names, and what usually follows is some sarcastic booing, tepid applause, or the sincere, enthusiastic screams of the ten fans of the opening band that came to the show.

But the announcement of the opening band is never ever followed by a lusty roar from a couple hundred people. Until tonight.

Chris and I look at each other in amazement as the tables empty out and fans (now there are female ones too) rush the stage. Francis, Ethan, and Ian walk out, wave, and rip into "Astroglide."

The difference between this and the last time I saw them is incredible. They are obviously high from the energy of the crowd, but they are not so high that they get sloppy. They are, as the musicians say, incredibly tight. They sound great, and they also look great. This is not only because of Ian's and Ethan's physical beauty, but because they appear to have a band uniform: they are all wearing black leather motorcycle jackets just like the Ramones used to wear, and plain T-shirts that match their Converse high-tops: black for Francis, red for Ethan, white for Ian.

The crowd goes crazy at the end of "Astroglide," and Ethan pauses for a minute, then says, "Thank you. We're Happy Jack, and my name is Ethan Walker Carrington the Third"—huge cheers at this, so I guess his "so uncool it's cool" gambit paid off—"and one thing I've learned . . . as a gay man . . ." More cheers, many of them female screams. Go figure. ". . . living in Boston . . ." You never lose with the hometown reference. He's playing the crowd with more skill than anybody in this band plays an instrument. ". . . so close to the Cape . . . is that . . ." And, knowing their cue in a way I don't, Happy Jack's fans immediately scream as one, "P-Town Sucks!"

I clearly underestimated Ethan's songwriting talent in thinking that this song had to be either a tribute or a put-down, because it turns out to be both. Francis, who can't really have strong feelings one way or the other about Massachusetts's gay mecca, is on fire— the full-on Dee Dee bass-playing slouch, Our Lady of Lourdes hopping up and down on his arm, the head bob—he is just so punk rock I can't stand it. I was worried that the lethargy and disinterest he'd been expressing this morning would lead to a lackluster per- formance, but he seems to have found his mojo, and he is tearing it up like a guy ten years younger.

After four songs, all three members of Happy Jack are sweaty and shirtless, and Francis steps to the mike, shields his eyes from the lights, and scans the crowd until he finds me. Then he says, "Thank you St. Bridget's Class of 1984. Thanks to Ashley for orga- nizing this. Make sure to stop by at the registration table and get your nametags. Here's one of your old favorites." The crowd is obviously baffled, though some are "woo"-ing along lest they appear not to get the joke.

I laugh—well, I suppose "cackle" is the right word here—and then get embarrassed when I realize my laugh is so loud and the crowd is so quiet. Now that he's invoked the class reunion, he can only play a song by Squeeze or the Cure, and his first four notes make it clear he's going to sing the Cure's "Boys Don't Cry."

My first thought is that this is just a much ballsier cover for a punk band than some Buzzcocks song, but soon I stop thinking about the career implications, and then I stop thinking altogether. Because Francis turns this slight, short song into one of the greatest musical moments I've ever witnessed.

First, there is the arrangement—the band is still super-tight, and they've obviously given this one as much rehearsal as the originals—and Ethan eschews the original's ringing lead and strummy acoustic sound for a huge, crunchy, distorted guitar sound.

And when Francis starts to sing, we leave the realm of good performance and enter the realm of something really special. He's playing his heart out, but where he sounded tentative and nervous singing "What Do I Get?" at Mister Punchy's, he sings clearly and passionately, like I have never heard him before. He's singing like his life depends on it. And maybe it does, for all I know.

By the time he gets to the first chorus, Francis's voice is shaking, and there are tears running down his face even as he's insisting that boys don't cry. It's just a song, a pop song, but it is something more to him, and, suddenly, everybody else.

Because the song, after all, is about screwing up, about being bereft, about being lonely and sad, and who knows more about these things tonight than Francis? When he gets to "it's too late and you've already gone away," he's got me crying too. He's shouting himself hoarse, singing to Lourdes, singing to Angie, singing to

God, maybe all of them or none of them, but he is giving the most intimate, raw performance I have ever seen. He's crying like a baby, and yet he is somehow managing to sing this song. He attacks his bass like he thinks it killed his wife, and I suddenly notice that the strings are red and there's blood all over his hand. By the time he finishes the last chorus, his voice is almost gone, his eyes are completely red, and the crowd goes into a frenzy unlike anything I've ever seen.

And when I say "the crowd" I mean even me and Chris. I am shrieking and Chris is roaring like he did when the Patriots won the Super Bowl, only much louder. There is no me, there is no Chris, there isn't anybody or anything except this music. We are not appreciating Francis's pain, we are inside Francis's pain. We are not enjoying the show; we are the show.

And, strangely enough, we continue to be the show. Ethan looks kind of stunned at Francis and at the audience, approaches the mike, and screams, "To hell with the Cardinal!" and away we go into a vision of angels with swords of flame carving up a corrupt old man. I think if he were here tonight, this crowd would probably rip him apart with their bare hands.

When Happy Jack reaches their allotted forty-five minutes and Ethan gives a "Thank you, good night!" the crowd roars and stamps, and after about thirty seconds, they come back for an encore, which is almost unheard of for an opening act. They play "I'm a Boy" and "Days," and they keep trying to leave, but the crowd won't let them.

"We're out of songs!" Ethan shouts apologetically as Happy Jack grabs their equipment and runs off the stage, presumably trying to avoid an ass-kicking from the headlining band.

The lights come on, the mix tape plays through the PA, and one third of the crowd leaves the club. I am guessing that Happy Jack will not be offered too many opening slots in the future. They have destroyed this crowd.

Chris is high as a kite and wants to stay to watch the headlining band, but I remind him how much the baby-sitter is costing, and we head home.

I CALL FRANCIS AT about ten the next morning. He gives me a groggy "hello" that lets me know I've woken him up.

"That was great! You were so great! I'm so proud of you! You were fantastic!" I'm gushing, but I don't care. I've been such a naysayer all along that I feel like I owe him a little gushing.

"Uhhh . . . thanks. It was great, I mean, it felt great from my end too."

"You just tore it up! I mean, really, that was as good a rock show as I've ever seen."

"Well, um, thanks. I'm glad you liked it. I really am. I got a little . . . well, I figured out why rock stars take drugs."

"Uh . . . why's that?"

"Because it's . . . I was so high after the show, and it . . . it was really hard to come down after that. I think maybe they get drunk or high or whatever because real life just can't compare. I mean, the show is over, and I'm completely in touch with everyone, I mean, whatever, the music is the medium, you know, the . . . it's like we're all mixed up in the music together. And then I have to put my amp in the van. It's a hard transition. So I stayed up all night."

"Watching TV?" I ask nervously. Remembering his months watching TV in the basement, before it was the bassment, I just don't want him to ever channel-surf again.

"Nah. I wrote a big apology to Angie, I mean, all my anger toward her just evaporated, like the music carried it off, and then I just felt like a dick. So I wrote this long apology. And then it was only two-thirty, so I went to the all-night Home Despot and bought some paint and tarps and got two walls in my bedroom painted."

"So when did you go to sleep?"

"About seven."

"Well, hell, Francis, go back to bed."

"My pleasure. Thanks for calling."

"Okay, sweetie." I hang up with a gigantic grin on my face and say an immediate prayer of gratitude. "Thank you, God, thank you for Francis, and for his happiness, and for Ethan Carrington the Third, and for the gift of music. Thank you for the healing it's brought him." I wish that Francis would pray with me. I know he'd say that if I'm thanking God for his musical career, then I have to blame God for his misery and for Lourdes's death. I can't argue with that—it makes perfect logical sense to me. But it just feels completely wrong. Besides—who else can I thank for this?

FRANCIS'S LIFE GOES crazy after this. Mine, thankfully, does not. Apparently there was somebody who owns some club in New York at the show, and he wants Happy Jack to do a residency for two weeks. There is a bootleg video of the show circulating on the Internet, and Francis uploads all of Happy Jack's recordings to various file-sharing and music download sites, where college students apparently start snapping them up at a great rate. Francis is pretty sure he can put together an East Coast college tour to bookend the residency in New York.

In the meantime, I tend to dying adults and two small living children. Chris and I get a regular commitment from our teen down the street and have several dinners out and actually see movies that do not involve wisecracking animated animals. Tommy starts kindergarten and loves his teacher. He makes friends with a boy named Rowan, and Rowan's parents come over for dinner, and we have a great time, and they make me laugh harder than I've laughed in a long time. Nobody in my immediate family gets sick, and nothing bad really happens.

I get a call from Mom and Dad one morning. I have been keeping them updated on Francis and the band, and Dad has tried unsuccessfully to download some Happy Jack songs to his computer, but either his computer or the Nicaraguan Internet infrastructure are not up to the task. I sent him a CD, but I don't know if they will have gotten it yet. "We're retiring!" Mom tells me.

"Uh, what do you mean?"

"I mean we're retiring. We're getting old, and we barely know Tommy and Dorothy, and we don't want to spend whatever time we have left thousands of miles away from you guys."

"Ack, Mom, don't talk like that. I mean, not about Tommy and Dorothy, about . . . about . . ."

"Okay, don't lose your mind, Clare, we're both planning on sticking around for quite some time, but we're not going to live forever, and we don't want to miss any more of our grandchildren's childhoods. It was really—you know that drawing you sent us, from Tommy's class? Well, I said to your father, we should really have a refrigerator covered in these things, we should be going to Christmas pageants, we should just be there."

"Uh, okay!" I try to process this in my mind, and I'm not sure how I feel about it. I suppose I feel several things at once. For one, I appreciate the irony of the fact that my parents have spent a great deal of time in the tropics and are planning to retire to the land of the five-month winter. I am also glad that they'll be able to know Tommy and Dorothy, that Chris's parents aren't the only grandparents they'll ever know, because I have been getting jealous about that. And, I'm terrified that they are going to end up being two more people that I have to take care of and be responsible for. And I worry that Mom and I will go back to acting like I'm seventeen again, which is what we usually do when we're under the same roof.

"Well," I say, "when is this going to happen?"

"Within the year. We're going to have to transition somebody else into the program directorship here, and it's going to take us a while to tie up everything. I'll let you know when we have a firm date, but right now we're shooting for six months from now."

"Uh, wow! Okay! That's great!"

"Yeah. It is. Okay, sweetie, we don't have much time here, and your father is mugging me for the phone, so here he is. I love you!"

"Love you too, Mom."

"Clare!"

"Hey Dad."

"Thank you for the CD! I love it! It's just so good, I'm so proud of him!"

"Yeah, it's pretty good."

"I told you he'd bounce back! I mean, I don't think any of us expected him to bounce in exactly this direction, but still, he bounced!"

"I guess he did, yeah."

"Your mother is, uh, less pleased than I am, because she thinks he should be teaching or something . . ."

"Yeah, I thought that too. But if you had seen them that night . . ."

"I know, you told me. It reminded me a lot of when I saw the Who in '67, or at least what I remember of it. I can't wait to see them play! Anyway, your mother is making those frantic hand signals, so I suppose I should go. I'm really excited about moving to Boston, Clare. We love you all madly, you know."

"I know, Dad. I love you too."

"Okay. We'll talk soon!"

"Okay."

*S*O THAT'S ON the horizon as something mostly positive with an asterisk, and overall, things are going very well. I mean, you could say that I have a perfect life. It's just that it's started to seem more and more boring. I feel old and boring, like I feel like this is it—I'm in the comfortable groove I'll be in until Chris and I retire, at which point we'll get an RV, go visit the grandkids, and die.

Or, possibly, we'll drop dead tomorrow. And then what? What if I'm there like Katerina with the bad liver, with my body shutting down, and my loved ones around me crying and some lady with a big ass there taking my vitals every day? Will I be able to look around and know I'll never get out of my bed and feel like my life was worthwhile? Will God be pleased with me when I die, or will everything good I've done be tainted by jealousy and discontent?

There's really no answer, so I try to suppress the little whispering voice that tells me that cool people are having fun even now when I lie awake in my bed next to my sleeping husband, and during the daylight hours, I'm usually so busy that I succeed.

And as long as I am in long-suffering mode, I apparently have to fill the Angie's mentor slot that Francis has left vacant. Francis has reconciled with Angie, but he's told her, probably wisely, that he needs to not see her in person for a while so he can get over his attraction, and then he's also very busy setting up Happy Jack's East Coast tour. So Angie calls me (!) to ask if we can have coffee and if she can ask me "some stuff about relationships and life and stuff."

I grit my teeth and say, "Sure, I'd be glad to," though I feel like some serious dental work might be preferable. So I tell her we can do that, but it has to be at a coffee shop near my house, because I am so busy blah blah blah, when the truth is that I just don't want to brave Boston traffic for something I don't really want to do.

She is waiting for me in the Starbucks up the street from my house. She looks uncomfortable sitting among all the suburban moms with their SUVs parked outside (no, I don't drive an SUV—Chris advocated one about a year ago and got a lecture from me about our responsibility to be good stewards of God's creation that I believe is responsible for peeling some paint on the stairwell). I realize with some shameful satisfaction that she's as out of place here in a suburban Starbucks as I was at the Mary's Cherry show in Cambridge.

I wave, order myself some kind of gigantic Butterscotch Hot Fudge coffee drink and join her at the tiny table.

"Hey," she says, "thanks so much for meeting me. I know this is awkward, and we don't really know each other, but I just . . . I'm about to make some major changes in my life, and I just wanted to talk it out with somebody sensible."

Sensible. I guess I'd prefer "incredibly cool" or "together" or "middle-aged but incredibly sexy," but it is a compliment of sorts. I guess.

"And," she continues, "there just aren't too many people who think straight in the music scene."

"I know," I say, "I used to be a serial drummer dater."

Oh, see, I was trying to bond, but now she's wearing this expression of complete shock, like it's just beyond belief that I was ever even close to cool.

"Wow! Really? But your husband's not . . . I mean, he wasn't . . ."

"No, I actually came to my senses." And now she looks hurt, and I feel bad. "I mean, you know, I wasn't actually dating the right kind of drummer, I mean, they were good drummers, but not really very good guys . . . I mean, I don't mean to say that you . . ."

"Well, that was actually the first thing I was going to ask you. I feel like I keep dating the same guy over and over, and he keeps pissing me off. So maybe I need to come to my senses. I mean, I shouldn't . . . Well, here's the deal. I applied to grad school all over the place, and I am thinking about, I mean I'm pretty sure I'm quit-

162 | Brendan Halpin

ting the band, and so I . . . I'm thinking about . . . I got into grad school in California. I only applied there as kind of a joke or whatever, I mean, you don't exactly need to go all the way to California to be a teacher, but I just thought, you know, out there having fun in the warm California sun and stuff." She laughs nervously.

"So, I guess, basically, what I'm saying is that I'm thinking about leaving my band and my boyfriend and my entire life here and just starting totally over, you know, go to California, let my hair go brown again, and just be a normal person."

"In California?" It's a cheap joke, but she laughs. We talk about her decision for several more minutes, but it's clear that she's already made up her mind, that she just wanted me to tell her she is not completely insane.

We end up talking for two hours—we trade drummer horror stories, and she tells me that Francis is her inspiration for both being a teacher and for starting her life over in California. "I had a lot of opportunities to do some really bad stuff when I was a teenager, and I only did about half as much as I could have, and I think that's because I got so much strength from going to youth group every week. It just . . . it helped me to feel like it was worth thinking about stuff and trying to do the right thing, which was kind of a foreign concept to me at the time."

We end with a big hug, and I give her a ride to the commuter rail station (she doesn't have a car! Why did I make her come all the way out here? I'm such a bitch!), and I end up sitting in my car outside my house for about ten minutes in the parking lot turning over the various ironies of this whole situation: Francis inspired Angie to be a teacher, she inspired him to be a rock star. Angie wants nothing more than what I have—a normal life—and I lie awake wanting to stay up late and play guitar and sleep with drummers.

I should go home, but instead I go to church. There are priests buzzing around preparing for the Saturday evening mass (the one you can go to and be done by seven, then go out and have a really re-grettable Saturday night and still sleep in on Sunday morning with-out offending God. Show me another religion with this kind of flexibility! I could never understand why everybody in college wasn't Catholic).

I'd like to be in some old, creaky church with incense-stained stone pillars, but I'm in my suburban 1970s-vintage church with the blond wood pews, wall-to-wall carpet, and semi-abstract stained glass. Still, I find the pew where we usually sit, pull the kneeler down, and kneel down and pray. I ask God to watch over Angie, to watch over Francis (not that God seems to need reminding of this—except for the part about his wife dying, God seems to hand Francis all kinds of interesting things without his ever having to do anything), and, most of all, to help me to be grateful for everything I have, to help me remember the awful Sunday morning emptiness of waking up hungover and smelling of smoke next to somebody who saw me only as a notch on his drumstick. "Please, God, help me," I say, and, for a few weeks, He does.

TRY TO FOCUS on appreciating the smiles of my kids (I know, it's like a bad commercial for snack foods or something, but they re-ally do have the power to liquefy me). I also focus on appreciating Chris, who has suddenly taken up chess with apparently very little success, and Italian cooking with, to everyone's shock including his own, a great deal more success. (He took a class!) Like my butt needs any more pasta, but dinnertime has become a time of usually good surprises and expensive wine, so I can't really complain. I also try to hear my patients and their families. I say a little prayer before I go into every house, asking for help being completely present for them and not distracted, and when I make a conscious effort (or possibly receive the divine grace) to devote that part of my brain that I usually reserve for worrying about or envying Francis to what's happening in the room, I find that I really like my work. This, the voice in my head (God? Chris? Francis? Mom? Dad?) reminds me, is no small thing, and I get to go home every day, even those days when I sit in traffic on 128 for an hour or some old man throws his lunch at me, and feel like I've done something worth doing. This is the way I always used to feel before Lourdes died and Francis's life went to pieces and I started feeling like I had to be the one to put them together.

And then Mom and Dad come to town.

And they start looking for houses, apartments, condos, anything, and find themselves priced out of almost everything.

And they stay with me.

And they reveal that they are back from Central America not just to see their grandchildren, but because Dad's been feeling really bad lately, really tired, and he's mystified their doctor in Nicaragua ("And the medical care in Nicaragua has really come a long way!" Dad exclaims), so they want some American medical care.

"Why didn't you tell me?" I yell at them when they drop this bomb.

"You just seemed like you had enough on your mind lately, sweetie. You've been really stressed out, and we just didn't think you needed anything else on your plate."

"Well, but, I want to know this stuff. You should have told me."

"Sweetie," Dad says, "I'm about ninety percent sure this is just some kind of tropical virus, and I'll be fine in six weeks, and I would have felt bad if you'd spent all this time worrying for nothing."

So Mom is alternately helpful and annoying, and she second-guesses my parenting decisions, and this makes me feel seventeen, though I was the one questioning her parenting decisions at that age. Dad does a lot of drawing and coloring with the kids, and he goes for tests.

It's at about this time that Francis and Happy Jack head off to New York, planning to play about half the colleges between here and there. Francis calls every day, and he is consistently euphoric. "We killed, Clare! It was even better than the show you saw!" or, "I felt a little tired before the show, and I was afraid it was going to be horrible, but it was fantastic!"

The band appears to be firing on all cylinders, and I am happy for him. He e-mails me links to all their concert reviews (when does he have time to do this stuff?), and aspiring rock journalists at every college on the East Coast exhaust their metaphor supply praising Happy Jack. And a week into Happy Jack's New York residency, three New York media outlets have described Happy Jack as "a must-see show," with one adding, "These guys kicked my ass and had me begging for more."

Because I am a happy suburban homemaker, I run out to the craft store and buy a scrapbook where I put printed copies of all the Happy Jack press, even the review that calls Francis "the scrawny but soulful bassist who inexplicably dedicated the unexpected rip-roaring cover of Squeeze's 'Pulling Mussels (from the Shell)' to the St. Bridget's Class of 1984." He loves that joke so much he can't stop using it even when I'm not there.

"I Wanna Get Married" is climbing up the iTunes list of most downloaded songs, though Francis informs me that Ethan is starting to feel like it's "a novelty song." Must be the Dick Van Patten reference.

Everything appears to be going great for Happy Jack, and for Francis, who sounds happier than he has in years every time he calls. One day he doesn't call at all, so I give him a call as I'm stuck in traffic on 128 at about 4:30, which I figure is late enough that he'll actually be awake, but early enough that he won't be sound-checking.

"Hey! I'm stuck in traffic! Tell me some exciting rock star news!"

"Oh," he says in this totally flat voice, "well, nothing much is happening."

"Whoa whoa whoa. What's the matter? You sound horrible!"

"Everything's fine, really. I'm just a little down."

I don't know if he wants me to pry or just assume that it's the whole dead wife thing kicking up again, but I decide to go with prying. "Are you just missing her? Are you having one of those 'this is not my beautiful house' moments?"

"I don't know. Sort of. No. I mean, it's not the fact of the band or the shows or anything, it's just that I . . . well, there's this girl, I mean woman really I suppose, but she seems like a girl, and she writes for some free paper down here, and she's been coming to the shows and interviewing us, and basically hanging out . . ."

"Yeah?"

"And so we ended up having lunch a couple of times, and I was kind of like talking about how I felt gross from eating out for the last three weeks, and she invited us to go to her place after the show for a home-cooked meal, even if it was dinner at one A.M., but you know we're big rock stars now so we can do that, but then Ian and Ethan bagged."

"Yeah?"

"And . . . well, she ended up cooking me breakfast, if you know what I mean."

"You scored! You scored!"

"Yeah, I guess."

"Francis, that is great! I mean, that's really great!" And I thought being in a gay punk band would preclude his getting laid.

"Yeah. I suppose."

"So what's the problem? Why do you sound so depressed?"

"I don't know . . . it just . . . it felt . . . I mean, yeah, it felt good, but she . . . I mean, she asked about whether I had a partner, and I told her I was straight, and I ended up telling her the story about Lourdes and my old life, and we were both a couple of glasses into this bottle of wine, and I started crying, and that's when one thing led to another, and I just felt guilty, like . . . I've become so trivial, you know, like everything she meant to me, everything my life with Lourdes was to me, is now some story I can use to get laid. It's like . . . I . . . I loved her so much, and I loved my life so much, and now it's like . . . it's so far gone it's nothing but a story, and I'm such an asshole that I'll exploit everything I ever loved just to get some. I kind of hate myself."

"I think you're being a little hard on yourself. Was your reporter mad at you or anything?"

"No—she made us waffles and sausage."

"Toaster waffles?"

"No! Real honest-to-God waffle-iron-from-a-garage-sale waffles!"

"Well, trust me on this from a female perspective, if she's whipping up homemade batter in the morning, she really likes you. A lot. So, you obviously didn't hurt her feelings."

"No."

"Are you going to?"

"I don't think so . . . I mean, I don't think we're boyfriend-girlfriend now or anything, or at least we won't be after I leave town . . ."

"Okay. So if you're not hurting her, you're fine. And Lourdes is beyond being hurt."

"But I feel . . ."

"Listen. I watch people die for a living. And I have never ever ever seen a husband as devoted to his wife as you were to her. And I've seen great guys, nice guys, guys who did everything they could for their wives, and every single one of them fell short of what you did for her. I was yelling at you to be less devoted, if you remember correctly, to think about yourself a little bit too, because you are also important, and you just sat there praying and getting smellier and hairier every day and surrounding her with your love every minute. So you never need to have a minute of guilt for anything having to do with her, pretty much forever. You earned a lifetime pass.

"And I reserve the right to nag you about stuff in the future, but you are the best person I know, so give yourself a break. And remember what Johnny Thunders said: you can't put your arms around a memory."

"So I'm supposed to take advice from a dead junkie?"

"Hey, you're the one with the 'What Would Dee Dee Do?' T-shirt."

He's silent for a few seconds, then comes back with a little, "Okay. You're the best person I know too."

"Well, you're nice and tragically mistaken, but thank you."

"So what should I do if she's at the show tonight?"

"Whatever you want. My advice is to ask her what's for breakfast tomorrow, but you do whatever's going to make you happy. You deserve it."

He tells me about some more good press, and then we hang up. Twenty minutes later, I've traveled a mile and a half in the direction of my exit.

HAPPY JACK FINISHES up in New York, and Francis tells me they have "major label interest" and he's thinking of signing a distribution deal with Sony, and promoters from all over are calling, and Fuse has picked up the video for "I Wanna Get Married," which some friend of Ian's apparently shot on digital video while they were in New York. He says he has a line on No Doubt's old tour bus, so they won't have to travel in the Element anymore. They have also apparently done a ton of press in New York, and so I should watch my newsstand for articles in *Spin*, *Blender* (whatever the hell that is), and possibly a cover story in *The Advocate*, or maybe *Out*. The writer, in addition to her other talents, apparently has "mad Web skills" and volunteers to maintain the Happy Jack "Web presence" (my brother actually uses the phrases "mad Web skills" and "Web presence"). I try to pry about the state of that relationship, but Francis is most certainly not talking.

Meanwhile, back at the ranch, or more accurately, the faux-colonial, my life is looking increasingly grim. Dad is able to go out and walk around, but he definitely tires quickly and he mostly just sits around listening over and over to the scratchy, quarter-inch-thick first pressing of the Who's *Tommy* he entrusted to me when they left Cincinnati. Chris offers to get him a CD copy, but Dad says the scratches are part of the album to him now.

So Mom and Dad are not looking for a house, and they will apparently be here indefinitely. They are sleeping in that weird extra room in the front of the first floor that we never use anyway. Chris insists that they need a door, Dad insists he can't impose on us by making us change our home around, and Chris eventually wins out, and he and Dad (whose role is mostly supervisory) hang a door that looks far better than it should given how much beer they drink while putting it up. After waiting three weeks to see a tropical disease specialist, and waiting another week for his blood work to come back, Dad has learned that he does not have a tropical disease. The doctors have ordered up a bunch more blood tests, and he's waiting for a bunch of scans. Nobody actually says the word "cancer," at least not in the confines of our home, but they've ruled out pretty much every kind of disease one can contract in Central America, so that's the next big thing they are checking for.

I am worried about Dad, and Mom is worried about Dad, and so

we deal with this as any two mature adults would, by fighting over
the kids. Mom is a habitual tsk-er, and so she routinely tsks over
what I'm feeding the kids, over what they are watching, and basically over my moral inferiority to noble indigenous people South of
the Border.

Things come to a head one Sunday afternoon when Chris and
Dad are at a Celtics game. Dad has never really liked sports, but he
really likes Chris, and he's happy to get out of the house for a while,
so Mom and I are home with the kids. I microwave some mac-and-
cheese for the kids while they are watching *Rugrats,* and Mom
starts: "You know, they'd probably like some nice rice and beans . . ."
She trails off here, leaving unsaid but understood about five more
minutes of lecturing about how it's so many steps removed from the
land, and something simpler would probably really please them.

"You can go ahead and whip up some rice and beans for their dinner if you want," I say, and Mom says, brightly, "Well, maybe I will!
Now where do you think I could get an earthenware crock?"

I'd like to tell her where she can put an earthenware crock, but
instead I call the kids in for lunch.

Tommy comes in and says, "Mo—om! Can I have the turbo-
charged RC rock hopper?"

"I have no idea what that is, but no."

"Aww!" This is not really a serious exchange—it's just part of the
Nickelodeon-watching ritual. But Mom starts tsking.

"Do you think they might watch something on PBS instead?"

"Mom, it's okay. This is just what we do."

"Oh, I know it is. I'm not judging or anything. But I think it's
worth sitting down with Tommy and explaining the mechanisms of
advertising, and the environmental—"

"Mom! He's watching *Rugrats*! It's not going to kill him! What do
you think Francis and I did every night while you and Dad were at
community meetings? We watched TV! A lot of TV! Would you like

to know about Kash Amburgy's Big Bargain Barn, or Tom Raper RVs in Richmond, Indiana? I can sing the 'Cut your costs at Kroger!' song! I can sing the Fifth/Third Bank 'Jeanie Can Do' song! I know who the Kwik Brothers are! I can sing about Tim Timberman and Jim and Chuck's Boot Shop, for boots and boots and more good boots! So stop! Okay, just stop! Just stop, for once!"

She runs out of the room crying, I start to cry, Dorothy starts to cry, and Tommy says, "Why doesn't Grandma like TV?" Because, of course, this is an incomprehensible position to him, which makes me think that maybe Mom is right and I have poisoned my kids' minds. Argh.

I wait a decent interval and apologize to Mom, and she apologizes to me and says, essentially, that she doesn't mean to be such a pain in the ass, but she's just so worried about Dad that she doesn't know what to do, and we end up crying about Dad again, and somehow we reach an uneasy détente with respect to child-rearing.

Francis and Happy Jack return to Boston, and I decide to invite the whole band to dinner. Dad is very excited to meet them, especially Ethan, because there is not a single person in this house or I suppose most of Central America who hasn't heard Dad talk about the Who, but everything he has to say will be fresh to Ethan, who, according to Francis, "Just listens to *Live at Leeds* over and over these days."

Mom and Chris cook up a storm, and Mom is so impressed with Chris's mastery of the cuisine of Italian peasants that she decides to make herself the sous-chef and forgo making any Central American peasant dishes.

Happy Jack arrive together, and I hug Francis, and Ethan says, "It's really great to meet you, but after hearing about you from Francis for so long, I'm a little disappointed that the halo isn't actually visible." I think I blush at this.

"Yeah, I keep it in the sideboard with the wedding china," I say.

Ian, being the drummer, gives a quiet, "Hey," and they enter. It is not five minutes before Dad is holding forth on the genius of *Quadrophenia*, but Ethan holds his own, saying that, in his opinon, the Who never recovered from the success of *Tommy*, and that everything post-*Tommy* with the notable exception of "Squeeze Box" is subpar.

We eat a lot of pasta and drink a lot of wine, and Francis tells us excitedly about some big shows they have coming up, and Dad just beams with pride. Mom is significantly more reserved, and finally busts out with "It's great that you guys are having so much success, but how are you giving back?"

There is complete silence, and then Ethan says, "Well, it's certainly my hope that as the band gets more mainstream acceptance, which seems to be coming, that we can maybe make it easier for gay and lesbian kids. I mean, I hope that we might be making it easier for kids to come out, maybe prevent a beat-down or two."

Mom is unimpressed. "But there have been gay pop stars before—like Boy Jim, or whatever. You obviously have this tremendous stage presence and intelligence, and I just wonder if there isn't more you could do with all of your talent."

Ethan shoots Francis a look that says, if I understand it correctly, "She's your mom! *You* have this argument!" so Francis steps to the plate and offers, "Well, Mom, first of all it's Boy George"—I'm so glad he corrected her because that was going to bug me all night otherwise—"there are different ways of giving back. I think we're doing something that helps nourish people's souls."

"But I thought you weren't going to mass anymore. Do you still believe in the soul?"

And now it's time for the hostess to step in. "Stop! We are not having this discussion in front of company! This is just not friendly festive dinner conversation, so the subject has been changed, and the new subject is officially . . . cooking! Chris?"

But Mom is undeterred. "Well, I'm just saying, if he's going to make some lofty theological claims for songs about lubricant, then we need to examine the theology behind it." I am now officially never letting Mom have two glasses of wine with dinner again.

Dad offers a tepid, "Karen, please," as I yell, "Francis, do not answer that. Do not!" I really am a strange kind of suburban matron. In every other house on my street, they would be horrified if tattooed gay punk rockers showed up for dinner, but I am horrified that my family can't muster the propriety to be polite in front of them. Chris would probably say that "propriety" is not something my family has ever been overly concerned with.

I don't know if Francis is going to respond to Mom or not, but Tommy fortunately saves the day with "What's lubricant?"

Ian nearly chokes on his linguini, Dad fails to suppress a smirk, Ethan sits there with his mouth open, and Chris coolly responds, "It's something you use to stop moving parts from rubbing against each other too hard."

Dad turns a suppressed snicker into a snort, which he then tries to disguise as a sneeze.

"Oh," Tommy says. "You mean like motor oil?"

And now Ethan is snorting, and Dad says, "Bless you," and he squeezes tears out of his eyes.

"Yeah," Chris says, looking pointedly at Dad and Ethan. "Motor oil is a lubricant. It stops the engine parts from wearing down, like we talked about when we got the oil changed."

"You can't let your lubricant get too dirty," Tommy says, "or else it doesn't work as good and your parts wear out."

"You got it, buddy," Chris says. My hero.

Dad and Ethan excuse themselves from the table, and Dad manages to snort out, "sneezing fit . . . allergies . . ." and they head to the living room, presumably to shake their sillies out.

They return, red-faced and smiling, about two minutes later, and the rest of dinner is uneventful, and Francis and Mom offer to clean up. Dad, Ethan, and Ian retire to the living room to listen to music, and Chris and I put the kids to bed. I read bedtime stories to Dorothy, and I think of nothing but hippos named George and Martha and their strange friendship for twenty minutes, and I am happy.

I want to go straight to the living room, but our house is not laid out like that, so I have to pass through the kitchen, and I hear Francis doing this angry whisper and saying, "Mom, if God gave a shit about Nicaraguan peasants, why does He make so many of them die of preventable illnesses? You have done way more for Nicaragua than God ever did! We're on our own in this world, Mom, and music connects us, and that is important. It is."

Mom looks like she's about to cry. "I know, Francis. I do. But I just—it breaks my heart to see you lose your faith."

"Me too."

I am tempted to jump in, but Chris saves the day again by arriving from putting Tommy down, and scooping me into the living room, where Dad is saying, "Yeah, Clare was into 7 Seconds, but they always felt derivative to me. I liked Minor Threat a lot better."

"But Kevin Seconds was really cute," I say, and we talk about music until Francis and Mom emerge from the kitchen looking as if they've resolved something.

So Mom and I appear to be cool, Mom and Francis appear to be cool, and Dad has decided to critically reappraise all of the Who's early work. Things go very smoothly for a while, and I even have to say that it is nice to have Mom and Dad here because they are forming really nice relationships with Tommy and Dorothy, and it makes me happy to see. It also makes me happy to have free babysitters in the house, and Chris and I even manage dinner *and* a movie without bankrupting ourselves on a baby-sitter.

So far so good, but there's always the question of Dad and his fatigue. And then it's time for him to go to the oncologist for his test results. I take the day off to go, and Francis walks over and meets us at the hospital.

He's late, so I wait on the ground floor for him while Mom and Dad take the elevator upstairs. Ten minutes after he was supposed to be here, I see him running down the street, little iPod earphones in his ears.

When he reaches me, I give him a hug that he doesn't really return. "You know, I was just listening to 'Apeman,' which is not really very PC, but anyway, there's this thing where he says, I swear I don't know how he did this, because what he's saying could actually be 'fogging,' which of course is what he always said it was, but if you listen to it carefully, he really hits the sound exactly between the 'g' sound and the 'k' sound, I mean it is completely ambiguous, it really could be . . . hey, do we have time for coffee? Where are Mom and Dad?"

"They went upstairs ten minutes ago."

"Oh, yeah, sorry. Okay then, I guess we should just go up then."

"Yeah." I'm really glad that we don't have time for coffee, because I think it might make him jump out of his skin.

In the elevator, he taps his feet, he drums on the panel with his fingers, and he keeps looking around like he's looking for another exit. I'm about to tell him to snap the hell out of it, but then I realize that this is the first time he's been here since they carried Lourdes out of this exact same hospital, so maybe I can cut him a break.

So we spend the entire ride up in the elevator with him twitching and drumming and telling me stuff about the Kinks. Once we get off the elevator, we see floor-to-ceiling windows with a nice view of Fenway Park. We walk through double glass doors that say

"Oncology/Hematology," and join Mom and Dad in blond wood chairs with maroon upholstery next to a tank full of yellow and blue tropical fish. Francis hugs Mom and Dad, then sits and starts drumming on the armrest until I lay my hand on top of his. He looks embarrassed and says, "Sorry."

"It's okay."

I look around the waiting room and try to play the game of which member of each party is the cancer patient. Everyone looks about equally worried, with the exception of a thin, red-haired woman and a short, goateed guy, who are snickering in the corner. The women with turbans, bad wigs, and head scarves are easy to spot as the patients (except for one woman who is wearing the full Muslim chador and so could go either way), but there are at least four groups of people where I can't figure out who's got cancer and who's just got terror.

Mom and Dad come back and pretend to read magazines for ten minutes, squeezing each other's hands white the entire time. Francis stares at the fish. Finally, a doctor who is young, petite, and Latina-looking comes out and says, "Mr. Kelly?"

Mom and Dad get up and Francis looks over at the doc, then back at the fish. "Do you guys want us to come in?" I ask, and Dad says, "No, sweetheart. We'll be okay. Just pick a good place for us to have lunch afterward, okay?"

"Okay, Dad. I love you."

"You too, honey," and he is gone.

"So," I say to Francis. "What do you think?"

"I think I want to talk about the Kinks some more."

"Okay."

"No. I'm sorry. I just . . . I think Dad's going to die. I don't see how anybody comes here and doesn't die, especially if I love them."

Dammit. That's what I was thinking.

"I'm afraid, Francis. I'm not ready for Dad to die."

"Me either. I hate this."

"Uh, listen . . . I . . . um . . . listen, I need to pray right now, and I would really like it if you would pray with me."

He opens his mouth like he's going to tell me why he can't pray, or why praying is for suckers, or whatever it is he wants to say, but then his face changes, and he says, "Okay."

I take his hands, and they feel cool and soft. "Have you been moisturizing?" I ask him.

"Helps the calluses," he says, smiling and closing his eyes.

I look around at the waiting room at the worried patients and family members and take a deep breath to get over my embarrassment. I close my eyes and say, quietly, "Holy Mother, please watch over our dad and mom right now and surround them with your love and care. Let them feel comforted by your presence. Amen."

"Amen," Francis says. Is he relieved that I didn't pray for Dad to be okay? I didn't do it out of any kind of consideration for him, but just because I can't ask, because I can't accept the fact that I might not get the answer I want.

We sit and watch fish for a while. I try to read about easy no-bake desserts for the holidays from a two-year-old magazine, but my heart's not in it.

Finally, the doctor who isn't Lourdes but who gives me a start at first glance comes out and says, "Mr. Kelly? Ms. Hayes? Can you come back?"

Somehow, in saying these words, she has lobbed a big stone into my stomach. I feel it hit, and I feel my stomach clench around it. Francis is already standing, and I know I should stand up too, but I can't. Because I know enough to know what this means. Dr. Not Lourdes is going to take us to a tiny room with a computer terminal and an examining table, one, maybe two chairs, and she'll say, "I'll just give you a few minutes," and I'll know from the tears in Mom's eyes what they are going to tell us, and then it all starts again.

I am possessed by the crazy idea that if I just stay in this chair, the events that are about to take place somehow won't happen, that I can avoid the gigantic chasm in front of me. If I never go into that room, Dad will be fine. Right? If a man gets a cancer diagnosis in a closed room, he doesn't really have cancer until somebody observes him, right? I think I learned that in a science class.

"Uh, Clare? Should I just go? Do you want to stay here?"

"No. I'll come. But you have to help me up." Francis extends his hand and pulls me up out of the chair. I find that in addition to the stone in my stomach, I appear to have had crucial parts of my knees replaced with a jellylike substance. I keep holding Francis's hand, and we follow Dr. Not Lourdes. Her nametag identifies her as Dr. Rosenzweig, Oncology/Hematology, so she's really really not Lourdes, and I am still thinking about this when she says she'll just give us a few minutes and Mom is crying, and the only thing that is different from what I expected is that there are three chairs.

This is good, because I need to sit in one. I start crying immediately, and this sets Mom off, so we are left with Dad telling Francis that he has actute nonmyeloid leukemia, and that he's beyond being helped by a bone marrow transplant, and so he's going to die sooner rather than later.

Mom and Dad still want to have lunch, and I am in a daze. I wipe my tears and shuffle to the elevators. Francis pulls me aside and says, "Do you need to go to my house and lie down?"

I am about to say yes, but I realize that what I really want to do is go to church. "I . . . I can't go to lunch," I tell Mom and Dad, and I sleepwalk over to St. Teresa's. I put a dollar in the box and light a candle and say, "Please watch over my daddy," and I go sit in a pew and sob.

I stare up at Christ on the cross. He's always there looking fragile and in pain in every Catholic church, because he's supposed to remind us that He suffered too, that our God understands what it means to suffer, that we're fundamentally not alone.

But even Jesus asked for this cup to pass from him, and this is essentially the content of my prayer when I can stop crying long enough to pray. "Please, Lord, heal my dad, I can't do it, I can't take care of him, I can't take care of Mom and Dad and Francis and everybody, I can't possibly do it, and I don't want strength to do it, I just want to not have to do it. Don't grant me the strength to do this, just make it so I don't have to. Please, please, please, Lord, please don't make me do this, don't make me watch my daddy die, I've watched a lot of people die, and I don't know if you're keeping track, but it's been a lot of people, more probably than a lot of people have ever seen, and all I'm asking for now is to not have to do it this once, because it's too heavy for me, it's too much, I can't possibly do it, I can't possibly do anything, please God, please."

I know God hears me, but He's terrible about returning His messages.

I stay there praying for a while, and I really wish I had a rosary. I just want to repeat the same prayers over and over, and turn the beads in my hands, and . . . I get up and wander back to the rectory, where Father Tim is in his office.

"Clare!" he says, "what a nice surprise!" And then, "What's wrong?"

"Uh, lots right now. I'm sorry, but I can't really talk about it. I'm just wondering if you have a rosary I can borrow."

"Of course!" He digs in his center desk drawer and pulls out a string of greenish white plastic beads. "Here's a glow-in-the-dark one. For those dark nights of the soul. You can keep it."

"Thanks, Father." And I return to my pew and, like an old lady, start telling my beads.

I am on my second trip through the Rosary when Chris appears at my side. I am so happy to see him I start to cry, and I think God must have answered my prayer and sent the only person I don't have to take care of here to take care of me.

He hugs me and says, "Francis said I could find you here."

I rest my head on his shoulder, and I am comforted.

Chris waits while I finish my second Rosary, and then he takes me home.

*M*OM AND DAD and Francis are there, and I head up to my room to sleep.

Chris calls to tell Helen I won't be in to work the next day, and I stay in bed. I feel guilty, because I know it's my job to take care of everybody, but the world somehow turns without me. Apparently there are discussions, and Francis comes up to see me at the end of the second day.

"Okay, Clare. We're hitting the road in two days, and you're coming with us."

"What? We can't! I can't! Dad . . ."

"Told me he'd disown me if I canceled the Happy Jack tour, even though I kind of wanted to. Anyway, we're doing a big westward swing. We're going to start in Burlington, Vermont, and then we have Albany, Buffalo, Pittsburgh, Cincinnati, Chicago, St. Louis . . ."

"I can't do that, Francis! I have kids, and Mom and Dad . . . we can't both run off!" I'm getting mad, because I want to, I want to flee and go on tour with a rock band and just pretend none of this is happening, but I have a job and kids, and I can't leave Chris alone with both kids and Mom and Dad.

"Actually, we can. Anyway, you can just come to Burlington and Albany if you want. Although I'd love it if you could come as far as

Cincinnati. Did you know they tore the Jockey Club down? I tried to book us there, but it doesn't exist! It's a parking lot!"

"But how . . . ?"

"Well, first of all, Mom and Dad are going to stay at my place, because then they can have the whole house to themselves. Chris's mom is going to come and help out with the kids for, I'm quoting here, 'as long as you need me.' And your job—"

"Francis, I've already taken more time off than I have coming to me! They'll fire me if I take off!"

"Yeah, because there is such a large pool of qualified hospice nurses out there. You're totally expendable."

"No, it's just that—"

"Listen. You'll ask for the time, and if they don't give it to you, you'll quit."

"What? Francis, I am an adult! I can't just do that!"

"Listen, Clare. I have a lot of money. A *lot* of money. And I think I'm going to get a lot more. We are ending our westward swing in L.A., where we're supposed to tape an appearance on *The Apples in Orange County*."

"What the hell is that?"

"Some nighttime soap opera that every teenager in America watches. We've got five soundtrack offers, we're starting to get checks from the downloads, and because we're the record company, we're getting a really big cut of the CD sales. Our Webmistress says the T-shirt sales are through the roof. They had a spread in *In Style* of all the celebrities who've been wearing them out shopping and whatever . . . "

"Did you just say the word 'Webmistress'?"

"Yeah, you know, the writer who—"

"You nailed." I finally get him to blush, which is a welcome change, since I am tired of being the one who's off-balance in this conversation.

"Anyway, my point is that I think I have a job for you, I mean, a real job, after the tour, but even if I don't, I am basically going to be swimming in money like Scrooge McDuck, and I would like to buy you a break."

"Aw, Francis, I can't just sponge off you."

"Why not? It's a time-honored tradition among family members of musicians. Come on—I need a posse, Clare, and every posse starts with a single hanger-on."

"Well, I'm not going to be your trim coordinator."

"My what?"

"The Beastie Boys had . . . oh never mind."

And so, after helping Mom and Dad get settled in to Francis's house and saying a tearful goodbye to my family, I find myself on No Doubt's old tour bus, with Ian behind the wheel, driving to Burlington as it begins to snow.

I've agreed to go to Burlington and Albany, being apart from my family for a total of three days, and only missing one day of work. I will be selling T-shirts, and taking a far less luxurious bus home after the Albany gig. The bus looks like an old Greyhound on the outside, and in the little oval destination window, there's a hand-painted sign that says, "Happy Jack." The equipment is all stored in the luggage bins below, and the inside of the bus is covered in orange shag carpet like all my friends had in their basement rec rooms in the early 1980s. There are two big couches that have that patina of grime that mark them as a thrift store purchase, a big table, a white dorm fridge that has also seen better days, and a big television. This is my brother's rock and roll tour bus. My dad has somewhere between six months and a year to live. Both of these facts are completely absurd. And I am sitting on a filthy couch in a gigantic bus with Motörhead's "(We Are) the Road Crew" booming out of at least six speakers that I can see, and watching Ian learn on the job as a bus driver. I wince several times as he brings the bus within inches of cars both parked and moving, and eventually I decide I have to just stop looking out the window.

Ethan plays some kind of video game, and Francis is just sitting and grooving to the music. He looks happy.

"So," I say, "this is what it's like."

"Apparently," he says. "This is really our first time in a bus of this magnitude. Usually it's me driving and Ian sitting in the back with an amp digging into his shoulder, and Ethan playing a GameBoy instead of the full PS2 setup that he has here."

"You look happy. Are you happy?"

"I'll be happy when I get to play. Right now I'm not really feeling anything. What about you?"

"I'm still freaking out. I'm so worried about Dad. I feel guilty for leaving him, and for leaving my kids. And I don't know . . . nothing seems to make sense. None of this was supposed to happen."

"Tell me about it. So all you can do is go with it."

Easy for him to say. He's long since adjusted to the idea that he didn't get the life he wanted, that he has no control over anything. Whereas I still mostly have the life I want, except that I just can't handle any more curveballs. I try my best to go with it. I sit back on the couch and pick up a music magazine, but this just reminds me of being at the hospital. I watch Ethan play his video game, which seems to involve a vampire wielding some kind of flaming sword, and it doesn't really interest me.

I don't really know what to do. I dream of time like this, where I'm not accountable to anyone, where I don't have to take care of anyone, and now that I finally have some, I have no idea what to do with it. Ian appears to have found his way off of narrow suburban streets and onto the Mass Pike, so I look out the window and watch the snow fall.

And it's falling harder now. It occurs to me that I never listened to the weather today, and I'm suddenly worried about whether this is the best weather for driving to Vermont.

"Anybody check the weather today?" I ask.

"Snow," Ian says. "Just a dusting."

Well, a bus like this should be able to handle a little bit of snow with no difficulty at all. So I sit back and watch, and the snow falls, and everything looks peaceful.

After about an hour, the sun begins to set, and I am getting really hungry. "Hey," I say. "What kind of snacks do you guys have here? I'm starving!"

Everyone in Happy Jack looks blankly at everyone else, as if to say, "I thought you were bringing the food."

"Uh," Francis says. "I guess we kind of neglected that particular detail. Ian, you wanna stop at the next service area?"

"Yeah. And thank Ethan for the fact that there's no food."

"I didn't say I was getting the food. I said do you want me to get the food! And you never answered!" Ethan answers.

Francis looks at me and rolls his eyes. "I was hoping a bigger bus would help with this kind of stuff," he whispers to me, and then shrugs.

Thirteen miles later, Ian eases the bus off the turnpike and into the service area. I get out the cell phone and call Chris. I tell him that I'm fine and that we are stopping the bus, and he tells me he's fine, the kids are fine, his mom is fine.

I call Mom and Dad at Francis's house, just to check that they are okay. Mom sounds delighted, it's been years since your father and I saw snow, your father is sitting at the window like a little boy, it's a wonderful blessing.

We stagger into the service area, and there are the usual assortment of haggard-looking families, teens who inexplicably don't seem to belong to anybody, and solo drivers lined up for coffee. The floor is brick-colored tiles, and ringing the tiny tables with attached swinging seats are a Sbarro, a Burger King, a Dunkin' Donuts, and a little convenience store. The red and green neon from the Sbarro mix with the harsh fluorescents and give everyone a slightly sickly appearance. One TV tuned to CNN hangs on the wall next to the Dunkin' Donuts, and the crawl on the bottom of the screen says, "PROMISING BREAST CANCER TREATMENT APPROVED."

I order a hot chocolate from the sullen clerk at the Dunkin' Donuts, and Happy Jack go to procure pizza. They return to the table, and the pizza is either incredibly delicious, or else I'm incredibly hungry. The weather guy on the TV bellows, "Just a dusting for Massachusetts, but Vermont and New Hampshire are really in for it."

"Well," Ethan says, "how do you rate our chances of anybody showing up for the show in Burlington?"

"I think kids in Vermont are used to snow. But I can call Brandy and have her send an extra e-mail to the mailing list just to make sure everybody knows we're showing up."

"Brandy?" I say. "Is Brandy your, uh, *Web*mistress?"

Francis blushes. "Yes."

"Brandy?"

"Listen, it's not like she picked the name. Not everybody can be named after a saint."

"I know, but nobody should be named after booze."

"Didn't you date a guy you called Jim Beam?"

"I never dated him, I only . . . anyway, I never told you that! How do you know that?"

"Altar boys know all."

"Jeez, you mean you . . . well, anyway, it's different, because obviously Jim Beam wasn't his actual name, we all just called him that because he was . . ." and now I'm blushing.

"Swinging some serious lumber?" Ethan ventures.

I can't speak, and my cheeks are on fire, and probably so red they're purple by now. Happy Jack have a hearty guffaw at my expense.

We contentedly munch our pizza for a few minutes until we're forced into eavesdropping by the people at the table behind Ian. It looks like a pair of parents and their sullen teen—she's got glasses and long blond hair, and very fair skin that is now all blotchy and pink around her eyes, where there are currently no tears coming out. She's wearing a blue letter jacket from Northton High School with white stitching on the front that says "Ann" and, underneath that, "French Horn." I know that school for some reason. Why does that name sound familiar? Northton is nowhere near where I live.

"It's been two years, Ann," the dad says. "I just think it's time for you to get on with your life."

"I'm sorry!" she squeezes out, and now the tears have started again. "It's not like I wanted this! It's just that being on the bus just made me remember—I just couldn't be on the bus without seeing his face, I just couldn't stay . . ."

"So we get a call from Mr. Marshall—do you know what went through my mind when he called, Ann? Do you know how panicked your mother was? So are you quitting band now? Is the whole thing just too painful? Can you play without thinking of Jeremy, or—"

"Jesus, Mike, let her be," the mom finally pipes up.

"You're really understanding, Dad, thanks. All I needed was for you to yell at me, and now I'm not sad anymore! Nice job!" She shoves some earbud headphones into her ears and eats her pizza in silence while Mom and Dad glare at each other. I am really glad I don't have to ride home with that family tonight.

We all exchange awkward glances, feeling uncomfortable the way most people do when strangers start sharing their intimacies in public.

"Okay, everybody, back to the bus!" I say, and Ethan grabs the pizza box and we all get up and head out the door. As we pass the kids playing the fighting video game near the door, I overhear a boy say, ". . . *is* Happy Jack, I'll bet you twenty bucks!"

When we get back to the bus, Ethan says, "Whoa."

"Yeah," Ian says. "What the hell was that about?"

Francis says, "I don't know. She couldn't stand being on the bus."

"Yeah," I say. "I don't know." Something's nagging at me, but I can't quite figure out what it is.

We have to drive slowly for the next couple of hours. Francis is sulking.

"Hey," I say.

"Yeah?"

"What's up?"

"I just . . . I used to help kids like that."

"Like what?"

"Like Ann in the service area. I mean, I just miss working with kids. Maybe Mom's right. It's just—I can tell Mom this work is important, but it doesn't feel like it when you see a kid crying like that."

"Well, did you see her jam the headphones in to escape her awful dad? Maybe she was listening to your CD, and it's making her adolescence bearable. Maybe you are to her what the Ramones were to you."

"Maybe. That feels pretty thin, though."

I don't know what to say to that, so I say nothing for a while.

Eventually we reach Burlington and pull into a parking lot at the college to set up camp for the night.

Ian gets out of the driver's seat and reaches into his coat pocket and pulls something out. Here, I'm afraid, is where the real rock and roll partying starts. But I'm here to leave my uptight, caretaking self behind, so I decide I'm going to have some of whatever he's having.

"You guys ready? I feel lucky," he says, and I see that he's holding a deck of UNO cards.

"You guys are going to play UNO?" I try to suppress a giggle. "You guys are pretty cool rock stars, huh?"

"Hey," Ethan says. "We play a buck a point. What else are you going to do when you have a whole day to spend at Dartmouth College or wherever?"

"I don't know. Bag some undergrads?"

"You obviously haven't seen the Dartmouth guys," Ian says, and Ethan says, "Anyway, this is an exclusive relationship."

So we play UNO, a buck a point, and I'm up two hundred bucks after an hour. I have to admit it does spice up the game, and I find myself screaming "You didn't say UNO!" at Ethan at one point.

The guys sullenly insist that we have to stop playing and get some rest for the big show tomorrow, so we take turns brushing our teeth and climb into our sleeping bags.

Just as I've settled in, I remember.

"Northton! Of course! Jesus Christ!"

Francis sits up. "What? What the hell are you talking about?"

"That kid. The crying kid."

"Yeah?"

"Well, I just remembered that I do know what she was talking about. Two years ago—remember? That band—she must have been there—the band from Northton was on some middle school band trip, and their driver fell asleep or something, and the bus went off the road and three kids died."

"Oh, God, that's awful." Neither of us says anything for a minute, as I'm thinking about that kid crying, and how of course she's crying, she probably watched Jeremy die when she was thirteen. I'd cry too. Still. Finally Francis comes back with "How the hell do you know that?"

"I think it's a fretful mother thing. I always pay attention to news stories about kids dying. I have to make sure my list of worries is completely up-to-date."

Francis laughs, and then he's silent for a minute. "That's just so awful. I wish we could do something for her."

"There are too many kids, Francis. Last year some kid killed himself in the cafeteria somewhere on the South Shore. Some kid in Peabody was killed running across 128 to get to the mall. Some girl in Danvers died just last week when her car—"

"Okay, okay."

"There are grieving kids all over. I think you might actually reach more of them with what you do now than by being a youth group leader."

I consider asking him if he wants to pray for Ann, for the friends of Allen who killed himself, for the friends of Janine who died trying to get to the mall, Melissa whose car hit a tree (I told you I pay close attention to these things), but I know what his answer would be. So I close my eyes and ask God to please, please comfort poor Ann, and her friends, and even her awful father, and Francis, and everybody else who's grieving, and by the way, while you're at it, could you make it so I don't have to grieve for my dad anytime soon?

I WAKE UP AT seven to find everybody else already awake. Some rock stars. Don't they know they're supposed to have a stressed-out manager who wipes the puke off them at noon and tells them they have to get moving? Apparently not.

The show in Burlington goes incredibly well. Whatever Francis's reservations about his current career, he's able to put them aside long enough to help Happy Jack level Burlington. I sell one-third of the T-shirts they've brought for the entire tour, so Francis calls and has more expressed to the venue in Cincinnati.

We roll into Albany late Saturday night. I call Chris, who tells me everything is going really well at home, and who wants to know how I'm doing.

"Well, I'm looking at my second night in a sleeping bag on the couch in this bus. I haven't showered, and I haven't eaten a vegetable in two days. The rock star life is quickly losing its glamour."

"Well, I guess that's good. I want you to have a good time, but not *too* good. I miss you."

"I miss you too." I think I miss the kids even more than I miss Chris. I am actually looking forward to getting on another bus in Albany tomorrow and going home where I belong. And then showering for an hour and eating nothing but raw spinach for two weeks.

Sunday morning too all of Happy Jack are up early. Ian gets a paper and some bagels, and we sit around the bus eating bagels and reading the paper. At 10:30 I say to Francis, "Hey. I'm gonna go try to find a mass. You wanna come?"

"Aw, I don't know . . ."

"Come on. What else do you have to do, besides lose at UNO? It'll probably save you a bunch of money."

"Well, okay," and off we go, wandering around downtown Albany looking for a church.

Eventually we find an old, poorly maintained Catholic church called St. Francis DeSales. It's gray stone on the outside with twin steeples and a big round stained glass window in the middle.

On the inside it's dim and dirty. It looks like it might hold a few hundred people, but there are fewer than thirty here, and Francis and I are the youngest by a good twenty years.

The priest, though, looks to be about my age, as is the music director, who accompanies the hymns on an upright piano in the front of the church. Francis and I can hear the music, but it's certainly not filling the space. It's like the congregation—it's here, but it's so small that it feels pathetic.

Still, the mass helps me to feel calm, though I do have a blip during the intentions when the priest says, "Lord, bless your servants who are doing your work with the poor in this country and in other countries." I don't need Francis to point out that Dad was doing God's work with the poor, and he's getting hosed.

I also don't need Francis to tell me that I need to get my ass home. Whether I'm right and God cares about them, or Francis is right and He doesn't, there are people dying who need my help, and while it sucks to feel like I have to be the one to take care of them, it sucks a lot less than playing UNO on a ratty bus all day and selling T-shirts at night, even if the music is good.

I go to take Communion, and, to my surprise, so does Francis. As we walk back to the pew, he whispers to me, "Does this taste like feet to you?" I snort, swallowing my laugh and trying not to spit the body of Christ onto the church floor.

The priest greets us with enthusiasm that borders on desperation as we leave. "New to the parish?" he says hopefully.

"Uh, no, we're actually just visiting," I tell him, and he looks crestfallen.

"Well, soak it in. This place is obviously going to be on the archbishop's list of parishes that are getting contracted."

"Oh. I'm sorry."

He looks at Francis. "You look familiar. Do I know you from somewhere?"

"Uh, well, I used to do some youth group work for the archdiocese of Boston. Maybe we met at a conference or—"

"Happy Jack! You're in Happy Jack!"

Francis turns beet-red. "Uh, yeah, well . . ."

He is uncomfortable, and obviously expecting the priest to give voice to his own doubts about the worthiness of his new career, but, instead, the priest comes back with "You guys are great."

"Uh, gee, well, thanks."

"This is obviously not something we can discuss openly, but many of my brother priests have downloaded your entire album. It's just so refreshing to . . . well, it means a lot to us. To me."

"Well, thanks! Do you want to come to the show tonight? I'll put you on the guest list."

"Wow, really? Yes, I'd like that very much. Of course, I'll have to lie to Father Pat about where I'm going, but it won't be the first time."

I am really afraid that the good father may be on the verge of some serious oversharing, so I pipe up with "I can set you up with a 'To Hell with the Cardinal' T-shirt if you want."

"Thank you, but I think that might be a little more daring than I'm ready for." Francis writes his name on a slip of paper, and we amble out to find our way back to the bus.

"See?" I tell him. "That's a sign that you're doing the right thing!"

"I don't believe in signs, Clare. It just means that one sad gay priest likes our music."

"Well, even still—the music touches people."

"I guess. But . . . well, I have an idea. I actually got it in church."

"What is it?"

"I'm going to think about it, maybe, I don't know, pray about it or something."

"Pray about it? Did you just say pray about it? What happened to God doesn't care about my problems?"

"I don't think God cares about my problems, or He wouldn't have given me the biggest problem of my life. But I always got into a better frame of mind—I mean, like I could think more clearly about stuff when I was praying. But I don't think that means God is listening."

"Well, I think He is."

"Well, I don't. But I may go through the motions anyway. I'll call you."

E SPEND THE rest of the day playing UNO, and by the end of the day I'm up another hundred and twenty bucks. Ian and Ethan are very glad to hear that I'm leaving the tour in Albany.

The show in Albany is just as devastating as Burlington, though the crowd is smaller and older. Happy Jack is simply incredibly tight. Francis pulls out Squeeze's "Annie Get Your Gun," and, of course, dedicates it to St. Bridget's Class of 1984. He really is never going to let me forget that. Oh well.

I sleep in the bus again, feel stiff and cold in the morning, and Francis walks me to the bus station. He gives me a big hug and tells me, "Send my love to everybody, but Dad especially. We'll be back in a month. I love you."

"I love you too. You're doing good work, you know."

"Well, you're doing better work."

I get on the bus and ride the three hours home thinking the entire time about Chris, Tommy, and Dorothy, and how glad I am going to be to see them, and how much it sucks to sit in a bus all day when you could be playing with your kids, even if they can't pay you a buck a point at UNO. As we hit 495, I am thinking about how great it will be to get back to work, how much more satisfying it is than selling T-shirts. By 128, I'm convinced that I will have all kinds of energy left over to devote to Dad, and that I can handle the fact that he's dying, that I can handle anything, that I am full of life and love and ready to do God's work. I say a silent prayer of thanks to God for my new attitude.

I get home and literally cry for joy at seeing the kids, and that night I attack Chris like he's the last man on earth. And my first week back at work goes remarkably well. After that, though, my great new attitude and energy is all gone. I am worried about Dad, I am worried about Mom—well, I am actually worried that she will stay around here forever and that our relationship will deteriorate to the point where we'll kill each other in some petty dispute about whether Dorothy can have a Cheez-It or something.

I have the Happy Jack CD in the car, and it's all I listen to during my workdays. One of my patients, a guy named Art who's about Dad's age and who has a bad heart and a really low number on the transplant list, dies in front of me. His wife is holding his hand when he just silently stops breathing. The family clusters around Art's bed crying while I call for a doctor to make up a death certificate and a funeral home to haul what used to be Art away.

Soon, I think, this will be my family crying, and my dad dying. And then Mom, Chris, Francis, and, of course, me.

Francis calls regularly with tour updates, and Happy Jack continues to slay audiences coast to coast. A prominent teen heartthrob makes a rather dramatic pass at Ian while Happy Jack is filming their appearance on *The Apples in Orange County,* and Francis apparently has to restrain Ethan from killing the kid, while the kid screams, "Not my face! Not my face!" Ethan writes a song called "Pretty Boy" that Francis says is "like 'Dedicated Follower of Fashion,' only more caustic."

And Mom and Dad live at Francis's house. We are over there all the time, and Dad slides gradually into inactivity. Mom puts on a brave face and says, "We're finally getting a chance to catch up on our reading! I'm actually up to books I purchased in 1995!" and then we go to make coffee in the kitchen and she sobs and hangs on to me and says, "I can't live without him, Clare, I can't possibly."

And I hug her, and I pray with her, and I tell her it's going to be okay. Because that's what I do. But I have the sneaking suspicion I may be lying to her.

The month crawls by. My family is over at Francis's house with Mom and Dad so much that we should probably just move in, and things with Mom actually seem to be kind of pleasant. At one point she says to me, "I just don't know if I'm doing this right, if there's something else I should be doing, if . . . we just have so little time left, and I don't want him to suffer, I don't know, I don't know if I'm doing it right."

"You're doing it right, Mom. Dad will let you know if he wants something different. If he's happy, you're doing the right thing."

"But I . . . should I be combing the Internet for experimental treatments? Should I call the priest who does the healing masses? Should I—"

"Does Dad want any of that?"

"He doesn't seem to. He mostly wants to listen to *Tommy* and see his grandchildren and read all the books he always meant to read."

"Well, then, that's the right thing to do. We have to go by what he wants."

Mom starts to cry, and that sets me off, and this gets to be pretty much of a daily scene in this kitchen, so much so that as the weeks pass, I find myself welling up every time I'm in the kitchen.

I don't find myself welling up when I'm with Dad, though. Compared to me and Mom and, indeed, most people I know, he's, well, happy. He runs the scratchy copy of *Tommy* through the big speakers in the bassment, he watches Tommy and Dorothy play, he talks to me about the books he's reading, and he seems to want for nothing.

Francis calls from the road every day, and Dad is always eager to hear about the details of the latest gig. Francis tells me he's got something big in the works, but he won't tell me what it is. He's got that same gleeful "I've got a secret" tone in his voice that he did before the construction of the bassment.

He asks me how I'm doing, and I say, "It's tough. It's . . . I came back from the tour feeling all energized, and it's like it's all gone. I feel fine when I'm with Dad, I mean he really doesn't need that much care, and he won't until he can't get out of bed by himself, and he's just . . . I swear, he's just . . . it's like we're all flailing around here, and he's just calmly waiting to go. So I feel okay when I'm with him, but then when I'm not, I feel like complete shit. All I want to do with my days is hang out here. I don't want to . . . I don't know. I'm not getting . . . I don't feel like I'm giving my patients what they need, or that anyway I don't have it in me to be as good at this job as I should."

"Well, do you want to work for me?"

"Selling T-shirts? No, I mean, I did enjoy taking all of you guys' money, but the work kind of sucked."

"No, no. We talked about this. I'll hire you to care for Dad. I'll pay you whatever you make from the hospice people. Or maybe I'll pay you more."

"I don't know, Francis, I'd feel funny about it. And anyway I don't know if that's going to work for the long term, I mean, as long a term as—"

"Listen. Don't worry about the long term. That's something I got from having my wife drop dead. But anyway, I've got some stuff in the works. I think . . . well, I don't want to say anything until it's finalized, but I'm making plans."

"For the future? But you just said . . ."

"Yeah, I'm full of shit. Anyway, please think about it. I think it would be a good use of this money."

"Okay."

I think about it for about a day. I tell Helen that I'm quitting. She begs me to stay, which should make me feel good, but instead makes me feel like a heel. I think about all the patients I'm leaving in the lurch in their time of need, and then I try to bury that thought as deep as I can.

And so I enter the employ of my rock star brother.

When Francis comes home, he stays with Mom and Dad constantly, except when I'm there. He disappears every afternoon for about three hours, and he won't say anything except "band practice."

Finally I corner him as we're on our way in and he's on his way out. "Francis, where are you going really?"

"I'm really going to band practice!"

"Right after a big tour? What are you practicing for?"

"We're writing for the new CD!"

"Why aren't you doing it at home?"

"Um, I don't want to disturb Dad."

"Francis, you know Dad would love it if he could sit in on your practices. What's going on really?"

He gets this mischievous grin. "It's a new project. That's all I can say."

The horn on the Element beeps, and Francis waves.

"Francis, who's in your car?"

"Uh, just a friend."

"What friend? Is that Brandy? Did you bring your girlfriend to town and hide her in the car?"

"No, it's . . . it's Angie, okay?"

My mouth hangs open for what feels like a full minute. "But she's in California, she's in grad school, and you . . . you're not . . . I mean did she?"

"There's nothing going on. We need another guitar to fill out the sound on our new project, she's on break for a month, so I flew her out here to sit in with us."

"What? You . . ." Well, it's going to be hopeless to get anything out of him. "When do I get to see the new project?"

"About two weeks. It's going to be great."

That afternoon, an engraved invitation arrives in the mail. It says, in purple ink, "Happy Jack requests the honour of your presence at the unveiling of their new project. Four o'clock in the Afternoon, January seventh, Two Thousand and Four in the Bassment of the Lourdes Kelly House." I think it's odd and slightly worrisome that he's calling his house the Lourdes Kelly House, but whatever. I try to make myself be patient for two weeks, since I'm clearly never getting the scoop out of Francis.

The next day I arrive at the house to find Mom engaged in a frantic bout of cleaning, like she only ever used to do if we had company coming.

"Hey, Mom! Who's coming over?"

"Nobody! I mean, well, nobody's visiting. We have somebody else moving in."

"You what?"

"Well, we met with Dad's oncologist today, pretty much to say goodbye and good luck, though he did write us a packet of prescriptions, and we got to chatting in the waiting room with Mr. Rodriguez, from the Dominican Republic. He's got an inoperable brain tumor and he doesn't want to die in the hospital, but his wife can't really be his caretaker, since they have three kids and she has to work. And there are no beds in hospice for him!"

"Yeah, that doesn't surprise me."

"Did you know that there are only twenty beds in hospice facilities in Greater Boston? Twenty!" I am ready to tee off on her when she saves herself with "Of course you knew it, what am I saying, this is your profession. But still, I can't believe that! And his insurance won't pay for him to go to a hospice facility!"

"Yeah, most of them don't."

"It's a disgrace! I've already called Mr. Cordero."

"Mom, there's nothing he can do for you. His company doesn't do health insurance."

"I know that, but I thought if he ever returns my call he could give me some names of people to harass about this. It's disgraceful, and I am going to make myself an incredible nuisance to any and everyone until something gets done. And, in the meantime, Mr. Rodriguez is moving in here."

I am stunned into silence for a minute. And then I get angry, because if Mr. Rodriguez is moving in here, that means I'm going to be his caretaker, which I suppose is what I get paid for, but this means . . . "I have to talk to Francis."

I stomp up the stairs and find Francis packing up his room. "Francis, what the hell is going on? Do you understand that there are regulations? You can't just open a hospice facility, which is what this is, you know, if Mr. Rodriguez moves in, and—"

"Relax, Clare. I've got it all covered. I've been conferring with the attorneys, and obviously we're going to have to make some modifications around here, but it's all fine. I've hired three other nurses too."

"You . . . you . . . where are you going?"

"Oh. I'm going to sleep in the bus."

And so, when I get my first paycheck, it comes from the Lourdes Kelly House, a 501(c)3 corporation. My job title is "hospice care coordinator." With four nurses and only two patients, my workload is laughably light, which is good, because watching Dad die doesn't leave me much energy for anything else.

The house, despite its current lack of patients, becomes somewhat of a hive of activity. Francis is planning art and music classes

for both the dying and their families, and special groups for grieving teens and kids. So there are always artists and musicians and social workers trooping in and out and being interviewed by Francis
and, when I have the energy, me.

Finally, the day comes for the unveiling of Happy Jack's new project. Francis makes us all wait upstairs while Happy Jack load in
their equipment. When we get downstairs, there are large, comfortable chairs waiting for Dad and Mom and the Rodriguezes and
no chairs at all for me, Chris, the kids, Aisha the night nurse, and a
handful of teenagers who are already sitting on the floor under several microphones on stands.

The drum kit is set up, and Ian is behind it wearing a long-sleeved
white T-shirt with a blue and red target on it. Arrayed on stools in
front of him are Francis with his bass, Angie with an acoustic guitar
and her natural brown hair hitting her shoulders wearing what appears to be a white mechanic's jumpsuit, and Ethan, who is wearing
a suede jacket with ridiculous fringe hanging down about three feet
from the arms, no shirt underneath, and a gigantic silver cross on a
chain around his neck that sits on his waxed chest. He's holding a
Fender Telecaster. Next to him is, I swear to God, Ann from the
Northton High School Marching Band, wearing her letter jacket
with the white stitching that says "Ann," and holding her French
horn. My first thought is what a weird coincidence it is that she's
here, but then I realize there can't be that many kids who play
French horn in the Northton High band, and Francis was really
serious that night in the bus about wanting to help her.

I know exactly what Francis is doing here, and I start to sob as
soon as I sit down. Chris runs his hand on my back and looks at me
quizzically. "It's . . . it's . . ." I can't even speak. This is simply the
best, most beautiful thing I've ever seen.

Francis leans in to his mike and says, "We'd like to thank you all
for coming. Dad, this is for you." And he counts a quiet "one, two,

three, four," and the entire band with the exception of Ann plays a few quiet, barely recognizable chords before Francis, Angie, and Ethan pick up the pace and Ann rips off the French horn lead that echoes "We're not gonna take it," and it's finally clear to everyone in the room who's ever heard it before that we're in the midst of the overture from *Tommy*.

I am still completely overcome. I look over at Dad, and he's wearing this gigantic grin, and Mom, like me, is weeping. Ann is really going at it with her French horn, and then Angie strums the unmistakable allusion to "Pinball Wizard," and I just start laughing uncontrollably while tears run down my cheeks. This is just the most audacious, wonderful, crazy thing Francis has ever done. The band segues directly into "It's a Boy," with Ann's horn sounding incredibly clean and pure, while Ethan's voice sounds delicate and beautiful in a way I've never heard before, but what's clear is that we're not just getting highlights from *Tommy*. This magnificent band is going to play the entire thing, start to finish.

And they do. I have seen this band (well, not this exact configuration, okay, but this band) several times, and they have always been incredible, but nothing, nothing could have prepared me for this performance. It's not simply that they show a range I never would have believed them capable of, from the quiet of "It's a Boy" and "1921" to the ass-kicking they administer on "I'm Free"; it's not just the fact that there's musicianship on display here that I've never seen from them before—many of the songs demand more than three chords and, God help us, shifting time signatures, and Ian in particular shows a virtuosity on the drums that I wouldn't have thought him capable of, getting Moon's manic fills almost right; it's not the addition of Angie's voice, which really helps sell the Mrs. Walker parts as well as "The Acid Queen," and which makes "Tommy Can You Hear Me?," which Francis, Ian, Ethan, and Angie sing a cappella, into something remarkable; it's not the very pres-

202 | Brendan Halpin

ence of poor Ann who can't stop missing her dead friends but who can play the shit out of that French horn; it's the fact that this entire thing is a present for Dad, who sits in his comfy chair the whole time wearing this blissed-out expression, occasionally closing his eyes and just nodding his head like he's floating on the music.

God love them, they even give us all nine minutes of the "Under-ture," which Ethan cited to Dad as specific evidence of the Who's inevitable decline, and which can charitably be classified as filler. Still, it's actually nice to get a bit of a break from the vocals, and as they play (and play and play) the "Underture," I think about how this piece is poking me in all kinds of uncomfortable places—the sexual abuse feels like it's dealt with flippantly (though Ian, whose voice is about two notches below good, does a great job of bleating the Uncle Ernie part in both "Fiddle About" and "Tommy's Holi-day Camp"), Tommy undergoes all kinds of unsuccessful healings, Lourdes wasn't healed, Dad can't be healed, Tommy's reaction to trauma is to become uncommunicative and stare blankly into a mir-ror, which reminds me uncomfortably of Francis himself, and of course my own son is Tommy, though I doubt that the Tommy who gives his name to the album was named for Thomas Merton . . . I know this is ridiculous, that this . . . this "rock opera," which is an oxymoron, ridiculous on its face—it's about a pinball wizard, for God's sake—this ridiculous, overwrought, overlong, overreaching piece of music today seems to contain all of our lives.

So it continues for an hour, which is incredibly draining, because I'm looking at Dad, who's all happy, throughout the whole thing, and I can't stop crying, I love Francis so much for doing this for Dad, for Ann, for Angie, for me. At the end of "We're Not Gonna Take It," Ethan, who's been singing the Tommy part, looks right at Dad and begins to sing the "Listening to you . . ." part. Soon every member of the band is singing to Dad. I can't vouch for the pres-ence of dry eyes in the house because I can barely see through my own tears, but I am sure I see Francis crying, and I feel Chris's shoulders heaving as he leans into me.

On the record, this song just fades out, but that's clearly not going to be an option here. ". . . I get the story . . ." everyone sings, and then Francis, tears running down his face, impales his amp with the pointy end of his bass. Ethan swings his Telecaster over his head and smashes it on the bassment floor. Ian, flailing with hands and feet, sends his drums and cymbals crashing to the floor. The sound is awful, percussive, screeching feedback, and I know I should be either wincing or rolling my eyes, because this should feel like a tame, canned piece of theater, like Happy Jack is the cheesy Who tribute band their name implies, but by God I want to smash some shit too. I guess it's contagious, because Angie is stomping her guitar to splinters and even Ann gets into the act, throwing her horn right through the head of the bass drum Ian has kicked over. It only lasts a few seconds, but it feels much longer, and then it's over, and Happy Jack and friends stand there, panting, looking kind of stunned at the destruction around them. Francis in particular looks bewildered, and it occurs to me that they really didn't plan this—I guess once they were actually singing this to Dad, it just became clear that they couldn't just end it. They had to break it.

So there they are in the wreckage of their instruments (and the mom in me is thinking that Francis better damn well buy Ann a new French horn, because those things are expensive, and that's probably a rental, blah blah blah . . .), and I look over at Dad. He grips the arm of his chair and slowly, slowly, tries to stand. Mom, who is a wreck, who looks like she's just been hit by a bus, which is probably exactly how I look, tries to help him, but he pats her on the arm and says, "No, thank you. I want to do this myself." And, all eyes on him, he stands and applauds.

We're all stunned for about five seconds while Dad applauds, but soon we are all on our feet, clapping, and Ann's friends from the

Northton High School Marching Band are screaming, and I'm screaming, and Chris is screaming, and we go on like that for probably a minute, and this, right here, right now, is my favorite minute of my entire life, as I'm outside myself watching this middle-aged lady clap and yell, and the sweaty, vaguely embarrassed-looking band members giving sheepish smiles, and Dad grinning like he's perfectly happy, and Chris with his arms around me, and Dorothy and Tommy running over to stomp on Angie's guitar. Right now in this place, with these people I love, with my ears ringing and my hands starting to sting, and my dad terminally ill, everything is fantastic.

Godlike.

Perfect.

Epilogue

AD DIES TWO MONTHS LATER. Francis made him a CD of Happy Jack's performance of *Tommy*, which he listened to every day until he died. At the exact moment of his death, Dad was listening to Ethan sing "Amazing Journey." I guess he felt like that was an appropriate way to go out.

Francis decides to release a CD of the performance simultaneous with Happy Jack's next CD of originals. The originals get rave reviews and sell or are pirated like crazy, guaranteeing a few more seconds on Happy Jack's fifteen minutes.

The *Tommy* CD, which Francis, over my objection, titles *Live at Lourdes's* (I tell him, correctly, that everybody is going to pronounce it "Live at Lords," guaranteeing that his wife's name will be mispronounced as long as the CD stays in print), receives reviews that range from polite puzzlement to disappointed hostility. Most people lament the lack of Ethan's wit and originality, and the reaction is summed up by this review from a local free paper: "While Happy Jack manages the difficult feat of pulling off *Tommy* live, a note-faithful cover of an album that's already been a movie, a broadway show, and, locally, a performance by the Boston Rock Opera is a profoundly pointless exercise. For completists only."

Of course, this performance was further from pointless than anything I have ever seen or probably ever will, but I guess you had to be there. The CD sells respectably, though, so perhaps some people get it.

Francis writes liner notes for the CD, which *is* a pointless exercise, since it will be downloaded in far greater numbers than it will be purchased, but they are very nice. I'm proud that he's my brother:

> This CD is dedicated to the memory of Stephen Kelly.
>
> Ann St. Pierre dedicates her performance to the memory of Jeremy Butler. Special thanks to all the musicians who donated their time and energy to this project, especially Ann, who destroyed a five-hundred-dollar horn without knowing whether we'd replace it for her. (We did.) It was an honor to work with you all.
>
> All profits from this CD go to the Lourdes Kelly House. The Lourdes Kelly House offers top-quality hospice care under the supervision of Clare Hayes, who is simply the best hospice nurse in the world. The Lourdes Kelly House is also the only facility in Greater Boston dedicated to working with grieving families, with a special focus on art and music groups, lessons, and classes for grieving children, teens, and adults. If you'd like to make a donation, go to www.lourdeskellyhouse.org and empty your wallet.
>
> The Lourdes Kelly House offers hospice care on a sliding-fee scale and never turns anyone away for monetary reasons. The scant availability of hospice care and most insurance companies' refusal to pay for it is a national disgrace. Ask my mom how to get involved in harassing your legislators and insurance companies by e-mailing her at Karen_kelly@lourdeskellyhouse.org
>
> Finally, a note to all of you who are grieving or watching a loved one die: there is comfort, and there is hope. You find it in the strangest places.
>
> —Francis

Acknowledgments

Thanks to everyone who read drafts and fragments and gave me encouragement and helpful criticism: Deborah Bancroft, Andrew Sokatch, Daniel Sokatch, Dana Reinhardt, John Andrews, and Kirsten Shanks.

Punk rock provided invaluable inspiration for this novel and invaluable assistance in the survival of adolescence. Thanks to all the bands who played the Jockey Club, but especially those that featured Karl Meyer, the hardest-working bassist in show business: Sluggo, the Edge, SS-20, and Human Zoo. Thanks to the Clash, Hüsker Dü, the Replacements, Squirrel Bait, X, and especially all Ramones: Dee Dee, Joey, Johnny, Marky, Richie, C.J., and Tommy.

Thanks as always to Doug Stewart for being exceptionally good at his job and for being my friend.

Thanks to Bruce Tracy, who helped me tremendously in making this book sharper and more accessible.

Thanks to everyone who helped on my long way back. Thanks to Suzanne Demarco for the sunflower.

About the Author

BRENDAN HALPIN is the author of the acclaimed novel *Donorboy* and the memoirs *It Takes a Worried Man* and *Losing My Faculties*. He lives in Boston with his wife, Suzanne, and their children.

About the Type

This book was set in Caledonia, a typeface designed in 1939 by William Addison Dwiggins for the Mergenthaler Linotype Company. Its name is the ancient Roman term for Scotland, because the face was intended to have a Scotch-Roman flavor. Caledonia is considered to be a well-proportioned, businesslike face with little contrast between its thick and thin lines.